ALL QUIET ON THE WESTERN FRONT

All Quiet on the Western Front

by Erich Maria Remarque

With an introduction by HARRY HANSEN

and with illustrations by JOHN GROTH

The Heritage Press · New York

The Book
That Shocked
a Nation

Early in 1929 there appeared in the bookstores of Berlin a novel
by Erich Maria Remarque entitled *Im Westen Nichts Neues*, which
dealt with soldiers' life in the trenches of Flanders and was translated
into English as *All Quiet on the Western Front*. There was nothing on
the surface to indicate that it differed from the dozen or more books of
war experiences already in print, that it would command more attention than Arnold Zweig's antimilitaristic *The Case of Sergeant Grischa*,
or that it would infuriate a large political party and lead to denuncia-
tion and exile of the author, and the public burning of his book.

If anything was arresting, it was the book's title. This happened to
be the final phrase tacked on to so many unsatisfying reports from
Great Headquarters, when it was well known that thousands were
wounded and dying daily. The French would reiterate in similar fash-

ion that there was *rien à signaler*, even when up to 100,000 *poilus* were in open mutiny. A veteran of the Great War, clad in ill-fitting work clothes, might stop short before a bookstore window as the title caught his eye and called up bitter memories. If he picked up the book and examined it, he was caught.

Evidently something like this happened. The novel, by an author unknown to the public at large, became the object of a whispering campaign among former soldiers and their wives. The German veteran, reticent by training and self-protective, was reluctant to reopen the past, but here was an outlet for pent-up anguish which made possible identification with its characters. The liberal journals, defying the brewing political storm, could assert: *So ist es gewesen!* – That's the way it was. Thereupon people in ever-increasing numbers put down their six marks ($1.50) for the book; the presses of the Propyläen Verlag poured forth 100,000 copies, 200,000, half a million, 700,000; and translators worked diligently to convert the text into twelve foreign languages.

Men were marching again in Germany in 1929. They had been marching in multiplying numbers ever since 1923, when Erich Ludendorff, the strategist who blamed his defeat on the home front, and Adolf Hitler, the fanatical top-sergeant from Austria, led the Beer Hall Putsch in Munich in a vain attempt to oust the radical government of Bavaria. I watched their followers congregate in Nuremberg in 1927, when they arrived all day and all night like migrating swallows, while I was making a pilgrimage to the Wagnerian shrine at Bayreuth. In the *Bierstube* of my hotel I asked a group at my table what their program was, and they replied with one of those circumlocutions so typically German: "*Dass müssen wir doch später feststellen*" – "That we will have to determine later." By the time Remarque's book appeared National Socialism was a powerful political force, identifying itself with *Heimat* (home) and *Vaterlandsliebe* (devotion to the fatherland), abstractions that have been used through the ages to tie the masses to military ambitions. These were Germans who announced, after reading *All Quiet on the Western Front*, that Erich Maria Remarque had slandered what they considered the finest ideals of their nation.

The book's quick popular success started inquiries into Remarque's credentials. It was learned that he was born June 22, 1898, at Osnabrück in Westphalia, the son of Peter Franz Remark, a bookbinder. He had broken off his schooling and volunteered for service before his class was called, and had been sent to the West Front when not quite eighteen. He had suffered a leg injury and recuperated in a hospital at Duisberg. After the war he had taught school and performed editorial duties on *Sport und Bild*. There was some speculation among his critics whether the spelling of his name, differing from that of his father, referred to some remote French ancestor.

Remarque told Axel Eggebrecht, editor of the *Literarische Welt*, that his novel was not directed toward any specific result. He said he had avoided expressing views of a military, strategic, political, social, or religious nature. Ostensibly he was as "unpolitical" as Thomas Mann, who was awarded the Nobel Prize for Literature in 1929. But this aloofness from the issues of the hour was exactly what gave *All Quiet on the Western Front* its narrative drive. Stripped of all digressions that might lead the reader into consideration of extenuating circumstances, the novel concentrated solely on helpless human beings, buffeted by chance, exploited by martinets, unable to exercise any intelligent control over their destinies.

This stark account of the misuse of civilized man seemed to be what the masses understood. There also were critics who welcomed Remarque's naturalism; and Walter von Molo, who had served as head of the Dichter Akademie, gave the novel superlative praise when he said that it was the monument to the unknown soldier. One may imagine, judging by later outbursts, how von Molo's citation aroused the anger of Hitler and his henchmen. Here, they asserted, was a man vilifying the undying heroism of the army. Moreover, anyone with Marxist, liberal, or neutral attitudes was suspected of opposition to National Socialism. Authors were considered the worst offenders, for even when they did not denounce outright, they spread doubt and skepticism. Better to eradicate their poison in the traditional method of purification, by burning. In the ensuing bonfires the works of Germany's novelists and thinkers went up in flames, Remarque's among them. Oskar Maria Graf, informed that his books would be spared, protested vehemently: "I demand that my books be burned!" That to him was a mark of honor.

Resentment against the novel was twofold – political and stylistic. Its enemies took to pamphleteering, for this was the period when National Socialism was laying a base for regimenting German life and thought. A writer calling himself Peter Kropp, the name of one of Remarque's soldiers, took up the attack in a monograph called *Clarity at Last About Remarque and His Book*. Here, he said, was an example of that cultural bolshevism that had for its aim the undermining of the healthy folk spirit. It presented completely pathological situations as normal, with the result that even intelligent persons would be taken in and lose their clear understanding of what was basic and healthy. He saw lacking a sense of the heroic, of comradeship, and of "the will to protect the homeland," which "obviously" animated every soldier at the front. (He did not know that trains bearing recruits to the front in 1918 bore scrawls reading: "More livestock for butchering by Wilhelm & Sons.") Kropp showed how deeply Remarque had affronted the war-minded:

viii

Can anyone undertake a description of the gigantic task that our front faced in its fight against a suffocating, overpowering might, without again and again being reminded of what is exalted and heroic? Can one picture to oneself any phase of the war, whether the heroic *élan* of our soldiers or the galling, teeth-clenching endurance amid shell-holes and barbed-wire entanglements, without coming upon heroism? Of this Remarque knows nothing to report.

Kropp closed his diatribe with a violent outburst: "Out of the schools with this book! Rise and fight, so that spiritual decay does not follow economic collapse!"

Remarque explained to Eggebrecht that his novel was the result of long brooding over conditions. He said:

> I was suffering from rather severe attacks of despondency. In an effort to overcome them I sought quite consciously for the cause of my depression. By this intentional analysis I came back to my life during the war. I was able to observe something quite similar in many friends and acquaintances. The shadow of the war hung over us even when we did not think about it. On the day this thought came to me I began to write without long reflection. This continued for six weeks, every evening after leaving my office. Then the book was done.

Many other German authors had written about the war, but nearly all had softened the impact of their realistic disclosures by taking extenuating circumstances into account, or considering moral and ethical issues. The author who came nearest to employing Remarque's objectivity was Ernst Johannsen in *Four from the Infantry*, described as dealing with the last days on the West Front in 1918. This appeared a year after Remarque's book. Here, too, was disillusion, and an absence of the patriotic preachment so eagerly sought by the conservatives. In the unrelieved blackness of their days, the men "fought and did not know why; they died without hope, without consolation, dully yielding to their fate."

Yet all the men who had reached the depths of despair were still able to wonder why they had been ground so low. They demonstrated that the German of the imperial twilight now recognized how he had been misused. Nowhere in civilized countries – certainly not in France, Italy, or Great Britain – was professional patriotism carried to so high a pitch as in Germany. A people of exemplary patience and endurance, proud of its cultural heritage, habituated to following a social élite, could accept as part of its destiny the inconclusive reports from Great Headquarters, the vacant chairs at the family table, the unending procession of widows to graves and memorials. All the visible evidence of the bankruptcy of national policy made no dent in the ingrained love of home and country shared by everybody who had passed through the discipline of German schools and military training.

There are no words in English that carry the sentimental connotations of *Heimatsliebe* and *Vaterlandsliebe*. "Love of home" and "love of country" do not properly translate the nuances of feeling in those concepts. They are expressed in many external ways. I recall a day of misty rain in a Belgian provincial town during the first German entry into Flanders. Narrow winding streets among tall plaster houses led like rivulets into the public square. From one of them came the sound of men's voices; a column of infantry emerged, pounding the cobbles, singing: "*In der Heimat, in der Heimat, da ist's so wunder-, wunder-schön*" ("In the homeland, in the homeland, it's so very, very beautiful"). It was emotion set to melody, fit to bring tears to the eyes. A critic of Remarque's drab setting complained that his soldiers did not know how to sing, and implicit in his criticism is this nostalgia for home, hearth, and "the land we love."

The violence of the attacks silenced neither Remarque nor his publisher. Both were impressed by the commercial success of the book and bestirred themselves to produce another – a sequel, of sorts. Re-

x

marque began pondering the plight of the veterans who had returned from the front and were trying to adjust themselves to civilian life. By 1930 he had completed the manuscript of *Der Weg Zurück – The Road Back –* and in April, 1931, it appeared in Berlin. Sure of sales outside of Germany, the publishers had arranged for its immediate translation into English, and it was published here in May of the same year.

But a true sequel was impossible, for of the original group only the voracious Tjaden had survived. Remarque needed a new spokesman and a new fragmented platoon. The survivors, however, differ little from their predecessors. They start home after a scattering of shots and grenades kills and maims a few more human beings on the eve of peace. (Something similar took place on the Argonne front, where lives were sacrificed while the embattled armies waited in their trenches for the official hour of 11 a.m. on that armistice morning.)

In the prologue to *The Road Back* there is a brief ironic exchange with members of the American vanguard, who want souvenirs. One of the Germans has found a box filled with iron crosses and now exchanges them for butter, eggs, linens, and money. Thus early in the story Remarque conveys a disdain for this highly esteemed token of individual courage, a hint that his antimilitaristic attitude still persists.

The returning soldiers and the people back home have little sympathy for one another. Ernst, the narrator in the sequel, affronts his parents by his behavior, his father by smoking cigars, his mother by coarse speech. Veterans who have preceded them, and have managed to find work in a bar or an office, disappoint their expectations of camaraderie. The women who fall on their necks turn out to be venal.

It was evident now that Remarque had a mission. The villain of the first novel had been the war – the senseless disorganization of society in which "peoples are set against one another and, in silence, unknowingly, foolishly, obediently, innocently slay one another." In *The Road Back* the barrier to understanding is the people back home, though here, too, the alienation of the soldiers plays a part. Remarque's sympathy is with the men. It also is possible that he has resented the accusations that he did not properly portray the courage and endurance of the soldiers in the trenches. He writes again in the crisp, objective style he used in *All Quiet on the Western Front,* only now he seems angry, ready to tell people off through his spokesmen, the maimed, disheartened, dead-tired – the wasted generation.

Most of the men were only eighteen when they broke off their schooling and enlisted. Now the community prepares to continue their education. After passing easy examinations the soldiers are permitted to teach on probation. Ernst faces forty children, the oldest of whom is ten. His task is harder than manning the trenches; the war has unsuited him for the simplest civilian duties. Toward the end of *The Road Back* the veterans are astounded to meet a new group of youths going through military drill with shouts of *Front Heil!* They recognize that the recruiting sergeants are again at work, and that the overbearing arrogance of the military is about to be repeated.

The only American war novel with the uncompromising naturalism of Remarque's book was *Three Soldiers,* by John Dos Passos, reflecting his experiences in a Norton-Harjes Ambulance unit in France and his encounters with military red tape. Dos Passos previously had written *One Man's Initiation, 1917,* which had no circulation. Disillusion and disgust also were strongly portrayed in E. E. Cummings' *The Enormous Room,* based on his detention for eleven weeks in a French concentration camp for some minor infraction of regulations when he was a member of the American Field Service. Most of the American writings dealing with the first World War were more entertaining than probing, and this was true of the most popular play, *What Price*

Glory? by Laurence Stallings and Maxwell Anderson, and Ernest Hemingway's novel, *A Farewell to Arms.*

When the war broke out there was a growing element of social criticism in American writing, but the popular preference was for the romantic. It was therefore logical that the first book to capture the attention of the general reader was *Over the Top* by Arthur Guy Empey, which dealt entirely with anecdotes of life in the trenches. But when stimulating books about the war began to come from England, the American public reached for them with eager curiosity. They included *The First Hundred Thousand* by Ian Hay, *A Student in Arms* by Donald Hankey, and *My Home in the Field of Honor* by Frances Huard. H. G. Wells profited by his comprehension of the moods of the middle-class Englishman — that is, himself — and with his superb journalistic sense produced *Mr. Britling Sees It Through,* which was widely read in the United States. From France came *Under Fire,* by Henri Barbusse, but Romain Rolland had to issue his strong antimilitaristic work, *Above the Battle,* from neutral Switzerland.

By 1932 Remarque had crossed the border to Switzerland and was out of reach of Nazi harassment. Obviously he and his publisher sacrificed valuable assets, but Remarque fared better than the Propyläen Verlag, for this was a subsidiary of Ullstein, which fell victim to the antisemitic campaign. Ernst Wiechert, who had pilloried the Nazis in *Die Majorin,* languished in a concentration camp. Many German and Austrian authors became exiles. Among those who came to the United States were Thomas Mann, Fritz von Unruh, Franz Werfel, Oskar Maria Graf, and Alfred Neumann. Stefan Zweig left his quiet retreat in Salzburg and wandered disconsolately in England and the United States, dying by his own hand in Brazil. Ernst Toller suffered a similar disillusionment and end.

Remarque was now established as a successful writer and his books continued in demand. For eleven years he lived in Switzerland, then moved to the United States and became a naturalized American citizen. He published frequently; a number of his stories moved with the precision of *All Quiet on the Western Front*, and contained characters battling man and fate. His most popular story after the famous war novel was *Arch of Triumph*, which also was filmed. He wrote *Three Comrades, Flotsam* (about refugees), *The Black Obelisk, Heaven Has No Favorites, The Night in Lisbon*, and a number of other novels. Returning to Switzerland in 1948, he made his home at Porto Ronco in the canton of Ticino (Tessin). In 1956 he wrote *Die Letzte Station* (*The Last Station*) dealing with the final days of World War II. Remarque's finest novel remains in print in Germany and Austria as well as in the United States, where it is frequently named on school reference lists. Other wars and their literatures have come and passed, but *All Quiet on the Western Front* is still prized for its convincing truthfulness.

HARRY HANSEN

ALL QUIET ON THE WESTERN FRONT

THIS BOOK IS TO BE NEITHER AN ACCUSATION

NOR A CONFESSION.

IT WILL TRY SIMPLY TO TELL OF A GENERATION OF MEN

WHO, EVEN THOUGH THEY MAY HAVE ESCAPED ITS SHELLS,

WERE DESTROYED BY THE WAR.

Chapter One

We are at rest five miles behind the front. Yesterday we were relieved, and now our bellies are full of beef and haricot beans. We are satisfied and at peace. Each man has another mess-tin full for the evening; and, what is more, there is a double ration of sausage and bread. That puts a man in fine trim. We have not had such luck as this for a long time. The cook with his carroty head is begging us to eat; he beckons with his ladle to everyone that passes, and spoons him out a great dollop. He does not see how he can empty his stew-pot in time for coffee. Tjaden and Müller have produced two wash-basins and had them filled up to the brim as a reserve. In Tjaden this is voracity, in Müller it is foresight. Where Tjaden puts it all is a mystery, for he is and always will be as thin as a rake.

What's more important still is the issue of a double ration of smokes.

3

Ten cigars, twenty cigarettes, and two quids of chew per man; now that is decent. I have exchanged my chewing tobacco with Katczinsky for his cigarettes, which means I have forty altogether. That's enough for a day.

It is true we have no right to this windfall. The Prussian is not so generous. We have only a miscalculation to thank for it.

Fourteen days ago we had to go up and relieve the front-line. It was fairly quiet on our sector, so the quartermaster who remained in the rear had requisitioned the usual quantity of rations and provided for the full company of one hundred and fifty men. But on the last day an astonishing number of English field-guns opened up on us with high-explosive, drumming ceaselessly on our position, so that we suffered heavily and came back only eighty strong.

Last night we moved back and settled down to get a good sleep for once: Katczinsky is right when he says it would not be such a bad war if only one could get a little more sleep. In the line we have had next to none, and fourteen days is a long time at one stretch.

It was noon before the first of us crawled out of our quarters. Half

4

an hour later every man had his mess-tin and we gathered at the cook-house, which smelt greasy and nourishing. At the head of the queue of course were the hungriest – little Albert Kropp, the clearest thinker among us and therefore the first to be lance-corporal; Müller, who still carries his school textbooks with him, dreams of examinations, and during a bombardment mutters propositions in physics; Leer, who wears a full beard and has a preference for the girls from officers' brothels. And as the fourth, myself, Paul Bäumer. All four are nineteen years of age, and all four joined up from the same class as volunteers for the war.

Close behind us were our friends: Tjaden, a skinny lock-smith of our own age, the biggest eater of the company. He sits down to eat as thin as a grasshopper and gets up as big as a bug in the family way; Haie Westhus, of the same age, a peat-digger, who can easily hold a ration-loaf in his hand and say: Guess what I've got in my fist; then Detering, a peasant, who thinks of nothing but his farmyard and his wife; and finally Stanislaus Katczinsky, the leader of our group, shrewd, cunning, and hard-bitten, forty years of age, with a face of the soil, blue eyes, bent shoulders, and a remarkable nose for dirty weather, good food, and soft jobs.

Our gang formed the head of the queue before the cook-house. We were growing impatient, for the cook paid no attention to us.

Finally Katczinsky called out to him: "Say, Heinrich, open up the soup-kitchen. Anyone can see the beans are done."

He shook his head sleepily: "You must all be there first." Tjaden grinned: "We are all here."

The sergeant-cook still took no notice. "That may do for you," he said. "But where are the others?"

"They won't be fed by you to-day. They're either in the dressing-station or pushing up daisies."

The cook was quite disconcerted as the facts dawned on him. He was staggered. "And I have cooked for one hundred and fifty men —"

Kropp poked him in the ribs. "Then for once we'll have enough. Come on, begin!"

Suddenly a vision came over Tjaden. His sharp, mousy features began to shine, his eyes grew small with cunning, his jaws twitched, and he whispered hoarsely: "Man! then you've got bread for one hundred and fifty men too, eh?"

The sergeant-cook nodded, absent-minded and bewildered.

Tjaden seized him by the tunic. "And sausage?"

Ginger nodded again.

Tjaden's chaps quivered. "Tobacco too?"

"Yes, everything."

Tjaden beamed: "What a bean-feast! That's all for us! Each man gets – wait a bit – yes, practically two issues."

Then Ginger stirred himself and said: "That won't do."

Then we got excited and began to crowd around.

"Why won't that do, you old carrot?" demanded Katczinsky.

"Eighty men can't have what is meant for a hundred and fifty."

"We'll soon show you," growled Müller.

"I don't care about the stew, but I can only issue rations for eighty men," persisted Ginger.

Katczinsky got angry. "You might be generous for once. You haven't

6

drawn food for eighty men. You've drawn it for the Second Company. Good. Let's have it then. We are the Second Company."

We began to jostle the fellow. No one felt kindly toward him, for it was his fault that the food twice came up to us in the line too late and cold. Under shell-fire he wouldn't bring his kitchen up near enough, so that our soup-carriers had to go much farther than those of the other companies. Now Bulcke of the First Company is a much better fellow. He is as fat as a hamster in winter, but he trundles his pots when it comes to that right up to the very front line.

We were in just the right mood, and there would certainly have been a dust-up if our company commander had not appeared. He informed himself of the dispute, and only remarked: "Yes, we did have heavy losses yesterday."

He looked in the dixie. "The beans look good."

Ginger nodded. "Cooked with meat and fat."

The lieutenant looked at us. He knew what we were thinking. And he knew many other things too, because he came to the company as a non-com. and was promoted from the ranks. He lifted the lid from the dixie again and sniffed. Then passing on he said: "Serve out the whole issue. We can do with it. And bring me a plateful too."

Ginger looked sheepish as Tjaden danced round him.

"It doesn't cost you anything! One would think the quartermaster's store belonged to him! And now get on with it, you old blubber-sticker, and don't you miscount either."

"You be hanged!" spat out Ginger. When things get beyond him he throws up the sponge altogether; he just goes to pieces. And as if to show that all things were now the same to him, of his own free will he shared out half a pound of synthetic honey equally among us.

To-day is wonderfully good. The mail has come, and almost every man has a couple of letters.

7

Kropp pulls out one. "Kantorek sends you all his best wishes."

We laugh. Müller throws his cigarette away and says: "I wish he was here."

Kantorek had been our schoolmaster, an active little man in a grey tail-coat, with a face like a shrew-mouse. He was about the same size as Corporal Himmelstoss, the "Terror of Klosterberg." It is very queer that the unhappiness of the world is so often brought on by small men. They are so much more energetic and uncompromising than the big fellows. I have always taken good care to keep out of sections with small company commanders. They are mostly confounded little martinets.

During drill-time Kantorek gave us long lectures until the whole of our class went under his shepherding to the District Commandant and volunteered. I can see him now, as he used to glare at us through his spectacles and say in a moving voice: "Won't you join up, Comrades?"

These teachers always carry their feelings ready in their waistcoat pockets, and fetch them out at any hour of the day. But we didn't think of that then.

There was, indeed, one of us who hesitated and did not want to fall into line. That was Josef Behm, a plump, homely fellow. But he did allow himself to be persuaded, otherwise he would have been ostracized. And perhaps more of us thought as he did, but no one could very well stand out, because at that time even one's parents were ready with the word "coward"; no one had the vaguest idea what we were in for. The wisest were just the poor and simple people. They knew the war to be a misfortune, whereas people who were better off were beside themselves with joy, though they should have been much better able to judge what the consequences would be.

Katczinsky said that was a result of their upbringing. It made them stupid. And what Kat said, he had thought about.

Strange to say, Behm was one of the first to fall. He got hit in the eye during an attack, and we left him lying for dead. We couldn't

8

bring him with us, because we had to come back helter-skelter. In the afternoon suddenly we heard him call, and saw him outside creeping towards us. He had only been knocked unconscious. Because he could not see, and was mad with pain, he failed to keep under cover, and so was shot down before anyone could go and fetch him in.

Naturally we couldn't blame Kantorek for this. Where would the world be if one brought every man to book? There were thousands of Kantoreks, all of whom were convinced that there was only one way of doing well, and that way theirs.

And that is just why they let us down so badly.

For us lads of eighteen they ought to have been mediators and guides to the world of maturity, the world of work, of duty, of culture, of progress – to the future. We often made fun of them and played jokes on them, but in our hearts we trusted them. The idea of authority, which they represented, was associated in our minds with a greater insight and a manlier wisdom. But the first death we saw shattered this belief. We had to recognize that our generation was more to be trusted than theirs. They surpassed us only in phrases and in cleverness. The first bombardment showed us our mistake, and under it the world as they had taught it to us broke in pieces.

While they continued to write and talk, we saw the wounded and dying. While they taught that duty to one's country is the greatest thing, we already knew that death-throes are stronger. But for all that we were no mutineers, no deserters, no cowards – they were very free with all these expressions. We loved our country as much as they; we went courageously into every action; but also we distinguished the false from the true, we had suddenly learned to see. And we saw that there was nothing of their world left. We were all at once terribly alone; and alone we must see it through.

Before going over to see Kemmerich we pack up his things; he will need them on the way back.

In the dressing-station there is great activity; it reeks as ever of carbolic, ether, and sweat. Most of us are accustomed to this in the billets, but here it makes one feel faint. We ask for Kemmerich. He lies in a large room and receives us with feeble expressions of joy and helpless agitation. While he was unconscious someone had stolen his watch.

Müller shakes his head: "I always told you that nobody should carry as good a watch as that."

Müller is rather crude and tactless, otherwise he would hold his tongue, for anybody can see that Kemmerich will never come out of this place again. Whether he finds his watch or not will make no difference. At the most one will only be able to send it to his people.

"How goes it, Franz?" asks Kropp.

Kemmerich's head sinks.

10

"Not so bad . . . but I have such a damned pain in my foot."

We look at his bed covering. His leg lies under a wire basket. The bed covering arches over it. I kick Müller on the shin, for he is just about to tell Kemmerich what the orderlies told us outside: that Kemmerich has lost his foot. The leg is amputated. He looks ghastly, yellow, and wan. In his face there are already the strained lines that we know so well, we have seen them now hundreds of times. They are not so much lines as marks. Under the skin the life no longer pulses, it has already pressed out to the boundaries of the body. Death is working through from within. It already has command in the eyes. Here lies our comrade, Kemmerich, who a little while ago was roasting horse-flesh with us and squatting in the shell-holes. He it is still and yet it is not he any longer. His features have become uncertain and faint, like a photographic plate on which two pictures have been taken. Even his voice sounds like ashes.

I think of the time when we went away. His mother, a good plump matron, brought him to the station. She wept continually, her face was bloated and swollen. Kemmerich felt embarrassed, for she was the least composed of all; she simply dissolved into fat and water. Then she caught sight of me and took hold of my arm again and again, and implored me to look after Franz out there. Indeed he did have a face like a child, and such frail bones that after four weeks pack-carrying he already had flat feet. But how can a man look after anyone in the field!

"Now you will soon be going home," says Kropp. "You would have had to wait at least three or four months for your leave."

Kemmerich nods. I cannot bear to look at his hands, they are like wax. Under the nails is the dirt of the trenches, it shows through blue-black like poison. It strikes me that these nails will continue to grow like long fantastic cellar-plants long after Kemmerich breathes no more. I see the picture before me. They twist themselves into corkscrews and grow and grow, and with them the hair on the decayed skull, just like grass in a good soil, just like grass, how can it be possible –

Müller leans over. "We have brought your things, Franz."

Kemmerich signs with his hand. "Put them under the bed."

Müller does so. Kemmerich starts on again about the watch. How can one calm him without making him suspicious?

Müller reappears with a pair of airman's boots. They are fine English boots of soft, yellow leather which reach to the knee and lace all the way – they are things to be coveted.

Müller is delighted at the sight of them. He matches their soles against his own clumsy boots and says: "Will you be taking them with you, Franz?"

We all three have the same thought; even if he should get better, he would be able to use only one – they are no use to him. But as things are now it is a pity that they should stay here; the orderlies will of course grab them as soon as he is dead.

"Won't you leave them with us?" Müller repeats.

Kemmerich doesn't want to. They are his most prized possessions.

"Well, we could exchange," suggests Müller again. "Out here one can make some use of them." Still Kemmerich is not to be moved.

I tread on Müller's foot; reluctantly he puts the fine boots back again under the bed.

We talk a little more and then take our leave.

"Cheerio, Franz."

I promise him to come back in the morning. Müller talks of doing so too. He is thinking of the lace-up boots and means to be on the spot.

Kemmerich groans. He is feverish. We get hold of an orderly outside and ask him to give Kemmerich a dose of morphia.

He refuses. "If we were to give morphia to everyone we would have to have tubs full –"

12

"You only attend to officers properly," says Kropp viciously.

I hastily intervene and give him a cigarette. He takes it.

"Are you usually allowed to give it, then?" I ask him.

He is annoyed. "If you don't think so, then why do you ask?"

I press a couple more cigarettes into his hand. "Do us the favour —"

"Well, all right," he says.

Kropp goes in with him. He doesn't trust him and wants to see. We wait outside.

Müller returns to the subject of the boots. "They would fit me perfectly. In these boots I get blister after blister. Do you think he will last till to-morrow after drill? If he passes out in the night, we know where the boots —"

Kropp returns. "Do you think — ?" he asks.

"Done for," says Müller emphatically.

We go back to the huts. I think of the letter that I must write to-morrow to Kemmerich's mother. I am freezing. I could do with a tot of rum. Müller pulls up some grass and chews it. Suddenly little Kropp throws his cigarette away, stamps on it savagely, and looking round him with a broken and distracted face, stammers: "Damned swine, the damned swine!"

We walk on for a long time. Kropp has calmed himself; we understand: he sees red, out here every man gets like that sometime.

"What has Kantorek written to you?" Müller asks him.

He laughs. "We are the Iron Youth."

We all three smile bitterly. Kropp rails: he is glad that he can speak.

Yes, that's the way they think, these hundred thousand Kantoreks! Iron Youth. Youth! We are none of us more than twenty years old. But young? Youth? That is long ago. We are old folk.

Chapter Two

IT IS STRANGE to think that at home in the drawer of my writing table there lies the beginning of a play called "Saul" and a bundle of poems. Many an evening I have worked over them – we all did something of the kind – but that has become so unreal to me that I cannot comprehend it any more. Our early life is cut off from the moment we came here, and that without our lifting a hand. We often try to look back on it and to find an explanation, but never quite succeed. For us young men of twenty everything is extraordinarily vague, for Kropp, Müller, Leer, and me, for all of us whom Kantorek calls the "Iron Youth." All the older men are linked up with their previous life. They have wives, children, occupations, and interests, they have a background which is so strong that the war cannot obliterate it. We young men of twenty, however, have only our parents, and some, perhaps, a girl – that is not much, for at our age the influence of parents is at its weakest and girls have not yet got a hold over us. Besides this there was little else – some enthusiasm, a few hobbies, and our school. Beyond this our life did not extend. And of this nothing remains.

Kantorek would say that we stood on the threshold of life. And so it would seem. We had as yet taken no root. The war swept us away. For the others, the older men, it is but an interruption. They are able to think beyond it. We, however, have been gripped by it and do not know what the end may be. We know only that in some strange and melancholy way we have become a waste land. All the same, we are not often sad.

Though Müller would be delighted to have Kemmerich's boots, he is really quite as sympathetic as another who could not bear to think

14

of such a thing for grief. He merely sees things clearly. Were Kemmerich able to make any use of the boots, then Müller would rather go barefoot over barbed wire than scheme how to get hold of them. But as it is the boots are quite inappropriate to Kemmerich's circumstances, whereas Müller can make good use of them. Kemmerich will die; it is immaterial who gets them. Why, then, should Müller not succeed to them? he has more right than a hospital-orderly. When Kemmerich is dead it will be too late. Therefore Müller is already on the watch.

We have lost all sense of other considerations, because they are artificial. Only the facts are real and important for us. And good boots are scarce.

Once it was different. When we went to the District Commandant to enlist, we were a class of twenty young men, many of whom proudly shaved for the first time before going to the barracks. We had no definite plans for our future. Our thoughts of a career and occupation were as yet of too unpractical a character to furnish any scheme of life. We were still crammed full of vague ideas which gave to life, and to the war also, an ideal and almost romantic character. We were trained in the army for ten weeks and in this time more profoundly influenced than by ten years at school. We learned that a bright button is weightier than four volumes of Schopenhauer. At first astonished, then embittered, and finally indifferent, we recognized that what matters is not the mind but the boot brush, not intelligence but the system, not freedom but drill. We became soldiers with eagerness and enthusiasm, but they have done everything to knock that out of us. After three weeks it was no longer incomprehensible to us that a braided postman should have more authority over us than had formerly our parents, our teachers, and the whole gamut of culture from Plato to Goethe. With our young, awakened eyes we saw that the classical

15

conception of the Fatherland held by our teachers resolved itself here into a renunciation of personality such as one would not ask of the meanest servant – salutes, springing to attention, parade-marches, presenting arms, right wheel, left wheel, clicking the heels, insults, and a thousand pettifogging details. We had fancied our task would be different, only to find we were to be trained for heroism as though we were circus-ponies. But we soon accustomed ourselves to it. We learned in fact that some part of these things was necessary, but the rest merely show. Soldiers have a fine nose for such distinctions.

By threes and fours our class was scattered over the platoons amongst Frisian fishermen, peasants, and labourers with whom we soon made friends. Kropp, Müller, Kemmerich, and I went to No. 9 platoon under Corporal Himmelstoss.

He had the reputation of being the strictest disciplinarian in the camp, and was proud of it. He was a small undersized fellow with a foxy, waxed moustache, who had seen twelve years' service and was in civil life a postman. He had a special dislike for Kropp, Tjaden, Westhus, and me, because he sensed a quiet defiance.

I have remade his bed fourteen times in one morning. Each time he had some fault to find and pulled it to pieces. I have kneaded a pair of prehistoric boots that were as hard as iron for twenty hours – with intervals of course – until they became as soft as butter and not even Himmelstoss could find anything more to do to them; under his orders I have scrubbed out the Corporals' Mess with a tooth-brush. Kropp and I were given the job of clearing the barrack-square of snow with a hand-broom and a dust-pan, and we would have gone on till we were frozen had not a lieutenant accidentally appeared who sent us off, and hauled Himmelstoss over the coals. But the only result of this was to make Himmelstoss hate us more. For six weeks consecutively I did guard every Sunday and was hut-orderly for the same

16

length of time. With full pack and rifle I have had to practise on a soft, wet, newly ploughed field the "Prepare to advance, advance!" and the "Lie down!" until I was one lump of mud and finally collapsed. Four hours later I had to report to Himmelstoss with my clothes scrubbed clean, my hands chafed and bleeding. Together with Kropp, Westhus, and Tjaden I have stood at attention in a hard frost without gloves for a quarter of an hour at a stretch, while Himmelstoss watched for the slightest movement of our bare fingers on the steel barrel of the rifle. I have run eight times from the top floor of the barracks down to the courtyard in my shirt at two o'clock in the morning because my drawers projected three inches beyond the edge of the stool on which one had to stack all one's things. Alongside me ran the corporal, Himmelstoss, and trod on my bare toes. At bayonet-practice I had constantly to fight with Himmelstoss, I with a heavy

17

iron weapon whilst he had a handy wooden one with which he easily struck my arms till they were black and blue. Once, indeed, I became so infuriated that I ran at him blindly and gave him a mighty jab in the stomach and knocked him down. When he reported me the company commander laughed at him and told him he ought to keep his eyes open; he understood Himmelstoss, and apparently was not displeased at his discomfiture. I became a past master on the horizontal bars and strove to surpass my instructor at physical jerks; — we have trembled at the mere sound of his voice, but this runaway post-horse never got the better of us.

One Sunday as Kropp and I were lugging a latrine-bucket on a pole across the barrack-yard, Himmelstoss came by, all polished up and spry for going out. He planted himself in front of us and asked how we liked the job. In spite of ourselves we tripped and emptied the bucket over his legs. He raved, but the limit had been reached.

"That means clink," he yelled.

But Kropp had had enough. "There'll be an inquiry first," he said, "and then we'll unload."

"Mind how you speak to a non-commissioned officer," bawled Himmelstoss. "Have you lost your senses? You wait till you're spoken to. What will you do, anyway?"

"Show you up, Corporal," said Kropp, his thumbs in line with the seams of his trousers.

Himmelstoss saw what we meant and went off without saying a word. But before he disappeared he growled: "You'll drink this!" — but it was the end of his authority. He tried it on once more in the ploughed field with his "Prepare to advance, advance" and "Lie down." We obeyed each order, since an order's an order and has to be obeyed. But we did it so slowly that Himmelstoss became desperate. Carefully we went down on our knees, then on our hands, and so on; in the meantime, quite infuriated, he had given another command. But be-

18

fore we had even begun to sweat he was hoarse. After that he left us in peace. He did indeed always refer to us as swine, but there was, nevertheless, a certain respect in his tone.

There were many other staff corporals, the majority of whom were more decent. But above all each of them wanted to keep his good job there at home as long as possible, and that he could do only by being strict with the recruits.

Practically every conceivable polishing job in the entire camp fell to us and we often howled with rage. Many of us became ill through it; Wolf actually died of inflammation of the lung. But we would have felt ridiculous had we hauled down our colours. We became hard, suspicious, pitiless, vicious, tough – and that was good; for these attributes had been entirely lacking in us. Had we gone into the trenches without this period of training most of us would certainly have gone mad. Only thus were we prepared for what awaited us. We did not break down, but endured; our twenty years, which made many another thing so grievous, helped us in this. But by far the most important was that it awakened in us a strong, practical sense of *esprit de corps,* which in the field developed into the finest thing that arose out of the war – comradeship.

I sit by Kemmerich's bed. He is sinking steadily. Around us is a great commotion. A hospital train has arrived and the wounded fit to be moved are being selected. The doctor passes by Kemmerich's bed without once looking at him.

"Next time, Franz," I say.

He raises himself on the pillow with his elbows. "They have amputated my leg."

He knows it too then. I nod and answer: "You must be thankful you've come off with that."

He is silent.

I resume: "It might have been both legs, Franz. Wegeler has lost his right arm. That's much worse. Besides, you will be going home." He looks at me. "Do you think so?"

"Of course."

"Do you think so?" he repeats.

"Sure. Once you've got over the operation."

He beckons me to bend down. I stoop over him and he whispers: "I don't think so."

"Don't talk rubbish, Franz, in a couple of days you'll see for yourself. What is it anyway – an amputated leg? here they patch up far worse things than that."

He lifts one hand. "Look here though, these fingers."

"That's the result of the operation. Just eat decently and you'll soon be well again. Do they look after you properly?"

He points to a dish that is still half full. I get excited. "Franz, you must eat. Eating is the main thing. That looks good too."

He turns away. After a pause he says slowly: "I wanted to become a head-forester once."

"So you may still," I assure him. "There are splendid artificial limbs now, you'd hardly know there was anything missing. They are fixed on to the muscles. You can move the fingers and work and even write with an artificial hand. And besides, they will always be making new improvements."

For a while he lies still. Then he says: "You can take my lace-up boots with you for Müller."

I nod and wonder what to say to encourage him. His lips have fallen away, his mouth has become larger, his teeth stick out and look as though they were made of chalk. The flesh melts, the forehead bulges more prominently, the cheek-bones protrude. The skeleton is working itself through. The eyes are already sunken in. In a couple of hours it will be over.

20

He is not the first I have seen thus; but we grew up together and that always makes it a bit different. I have copied his essays. At school he used to wear a brown coat with a belt and shiny sleeves. He was the only one of us, too, who could do the giant's turn on the parallel bars. His hair flew in his face like silk when he did it. Kantorek was proud of him for it. But he couldn't endure cigarettes. His skin was very white; he had something of the girl about him.

I glance at my boots. They are big and clumsy, the breeches are tucked into them, and standing up one looks well-built and powerful in these great drain-pipes. But when we go bathing and strip, suddenly we have slender legs again and slight shoulders. We are no longer soldiers but little more than boys; no one would believe that we could carry packs. It is a strange moment when we stand naked; then we become civilians, and almost feel ourselves to be so. When bathing Franz Kemmerich looked as slight and frail as a child. There he lies now – but why? The whole world ought to pass by this bed and say: "That is Franz Kemmerich, nineteen and a half years old, he doesn't want to die. Let him not die!"

My thoughts become confused. This atmosphere of carbolic and gangrene clogs the lungs, it is a thick gruel, it suffocates.

It grows dark. Kemmerich's face changes colour, it lifts from the pillow and is so pale that it gleams. The mouth moves slightly. I draw near to him. He whispers: "If you find my watch, send it home –"

I do not reply. It is no use any more. No one can console him. I am wretched with helplessness. This forehead with its hollow temples, this mouth that is now merely a slit, this sharp nose! And the fat, weeping woman at home to whom I must write. If only the letter were sent off already!

Hospital-orderlies go to and fro with bottles and pails. One of them comes up, casts a glance at Kemmerich and goes away again. You can see he is waiting, apparently he wants the bed.

I bend over Franz and talk to him as though that could save him: "Perhaps you will go to the convalescent home at Klosterberg, among the villas, Franz. Then you can look out from the window across the fields to the two trees on the horizon. It is the loveliest time of the year now, when the corn ripens; at evening the fields in the sunlight look like mother-of-pearl. And the lane of poplars by the Klosterbach, where we used to catch sticklebacks! You can build an aquarium again and keep fish in it, and you can go out without asking anyone, you can even play the piano if you want to."

I lean down over his face which lies in the shadow. He still breathes, lightly. His face is wet, he is crying. What a fine mess I have made of it with my foolish talk!

"But Franz" – I put my arm round his shoulders and put my face against his. "Will you sleep now?"

He does not answer. The tears run down his cheeks. I would like to wipe them away but my handkerchief is too dirty.

An hour passes. I sit tensely and watch his every movement in case he may perhaps say something. What if he were to open his mouth and cry out! But he only weeps, his head turned aside. He does not speak of his mother or his brothers and sisters. He says nothing; all that lies behind him; he is entirely alone now with his little life of nineteen years, and cries because it leaves him. This is the most disturbing and hardest parting that ever I have seen, although it was pretty bad too with Tiedjen, who called for his mother – a big bear of a fellow who, with wild eyes full of terror, held off the doctor from his bed with a dagger until he collapsed.

Suddenly Kemmerich groans and begins to gurgle.

I jump up, stumble outside and demand: "Where is the doctor? Where is the doctor?"

As I catch sight of the white apron I seize hold of it: "Come quick, Franz Kemmerich is dying."

22

He frees himself and asks an orderly standing by: "Which will that be?"

He says: "Bed 26, amputated thigh."

He sniffs: "How should I know anything about it, I've amputated five legs to-day"; he shoves me away, says to the hospital-orderly, "You see to it," and runs off to the operating room.

I tremble with rage as I go along with the orderly. The man looks at me and says: "One operation after another since five o'clock this morning. You know to-day alone there have been sixteen deaths – yours is the seventeenth. There will probably be twenty altogether –"

I become faint, all at once I cannot do any more. I won't revile any more, it is senseless, I could drop down and never rise up again.

We are by Kemmerich's bed. He is dead. The face is still wet from the tears. The eyes are half open and yellow like old horn buttons.

The orderly pokes me in the ribs. "Are you taking his things with you?" I nod.

He goes on. "We must take him away at once, we want the bed. Outside they are lying on the floor."

I collect the things, untie Kemmerich's identification disc and take it away. The orderly asks about the pay-book. I say that it is probably in the Orderly Room, and go. Behind me they are already hauling Franz on to a waterproof sheet.

Outside the door I am aware of the darkness and the wind as a deliverance. I breathe as deep as I can, and feel the breeze in my face, warm and soft as never before. Thoughts of girls, of flowery meadows, of white clouds suddenly come into my head. My feet begin to move forward in my boots, I go quicker, I run. Soldiers pass by me, I hear their voices without understanding. The earth is streaming with forces which pour into me through the soles of my feet. The night crackles electrically, the front thunders like a concert of drums. My limbs move supplely, I feel my joints strong, I breathe the air deeply. The night lives, I live. I feel a hunger, greater than comes from the belly alone.

Müller stands in front of the hut and waits for me. I give him the boots. We go in and he tries them on. They fit well.

He roots among his supplies and offers me a fine piece of saveloy. With it goes hot tea and rum.

Chapter Three

Reinforcements have arrived. The vacancies have been filled and the sacks of straw are already laid out in the huts. Some of them are old hands but there are twenty-five men of a later draft from the base. They are about two years younger than us. Kropp nudges me: "Seen the infants?"

I nod. We stick out our chests, shave in the open, shove our hands in our pockets, inspect the recruits and feel ourselves to be stone-age veterans.

Katczinsky joins us. We stroll past the horse-boxes and go over to the reinforcements, who have already been supplied with gas-masks and coffee.

"Long time since you've had anything decent to eat, eh?" Kat asks one of the youngsters.

He grimaces. "For breakfast, turnip-bread — lunch, turnip-stew — supper, turnip-cutlets and turnip-salad." Kat gives a knowing whistle.

"Bread made of turnips? You've been in luck, it's nothing new for it to be made of sawdust. But what do you say to haricot beans? Have some?"

The youngster turns red: "You can't kid me."

Katczinsky merely says: "Fetch your mess-tin."

We follow curiously. He takes us to a tub beside his straw sack. It is nearly half full of a stew of beef and beans. Katczinsky plants himself in front of it like a general and says:

"Sharp eyes and light fingers! That's what the Prussians say."

We are surprised. "Great guts, Kat, how did you come by that?" I ask him.

"Ginger was glad I took it. I gave him three pieces of parachute silk for it. Cold beans taste fine, too."

Grudgingly he gives the youngster a portion and says:

"Next time you come with your mess-tin have a cigar or a chew of tobacco in your other hand. Get me?" Then he turns to us. "You get off scot free, of course."

Katczinsky never goes short; he has a sixth sense. There are such people everywhere but one does not appreciate it at first. Every company has one or two. Katczinsky is the smartest I know. By trade he is a cobbler, I believe, but that hasn't anything to do with it; he understands all trades. It's a good thing to be friends with him, as Kropp and I are, and Haie Westhus too, more or less. But Haie is rather the executive arm operating under Kat's orders when things come to blows. For that he has his qualifications.

For example, we land at night in some entirely unknown spot, a sorry hole, that has been eaten out to the very walls. We are quartered in a small dark factory adapted to the purpose. There are beds in it, or rather bunks – a couple of wooden beams over which wire netting is stretched.

Wire netting is hard. And there's nothing to put on it. Our waterproof sheets are too thin. We use our blankets to cover ourselves.

Kat looks at the place and then says to Haie Westhus: "Come with me." They go off to explore. Half an hour later they are back again with arms full of straw. Kat has found a horse-box with straw in it. Now we might sleep if we weren't so terribly hungry.

Kropp asks an artilleryman who has been some time in this neighbourhood: "Is there a canteen anywhere abouts?"

"Is there a what?" he laughs. "There's nothing to be had here. You won't find so much as a crust of bread here."

"Aren't there any inhabitants here at all then?"

He spits. "Yes, a couple. But they mostly loaf round the cook-house and beg."

"That's a bad business! – Then we'll have to pull in our belts and wait till the rations come up in the morning."

But I see Kat has put on his cap.

"Where to, Kat?" I ask.

"Just to explore the place a bit." He strolls off. The artilleryman grins scornfully. "Let him explore! But don't be too hopeful about it."

Disappointed we lie down and consider whether we couldn't have a go at the iron rations. But it's too risky; so we try to get a wink of sleep.

Kropp divides a cigarette and hands me half. Tjaden gives an account of his national dish – broad-beans and bacon. He despises it when not flavoured with bog-myrtle, and, "for God's sake, let it all be cooked together, not the potatoes, the beans, and the bacon separately." Someone growls that he will pound Tjaden into bog-myrtle

27

if he doesn't shut up. Then all becomes quiet in the big room – only the candles flickering from the necks of a couple of bottles and the artilleryman spitting every now and then.

We stir a bit as the door opens and Kat appears. I think I must be dreaming; he has two loaves of bread under his arm and a blood-stained sandbag full of horse-flesh in his hand.

The artilleryman's pipe drops from his mouth. He feels the bread. "Real bread, by God! and still hot too!"

Kat gives no explanation. He has the bread, the rest doesn't matter. I'm sure that if he were planted down in the middle of the desert, in half an hour he would have gathered together a supper of roast meat, dates, and wine.

"Cut some wood," he says curtly to Haie.

Then he hauls out a frying-pan from under his coat, and a handful of salt as well as a lump of fat from his pocket. He has thought of everything. Haie makes a fire on the floor. It lights up the empty room of the factory. We climb out of bed.

The artilleryman hesitates. He wonders whether to praise Kat and so perhaps gain a little for himself. But Katczinsky doesn't even see him, he might as well be thin air. He goes off cursing.

Kat knows the way to roast horse-flesh so that it's tender. It shouldn't be put straight into the pan, that makes it tough. It should be boiled first in a little water. With our knives we squat round in a circle and fill our bellies.

That is Kat. If for but one hour in a year something eatable were to be had in some one place only, within that hour, as if moved by a vision, he would put on his cap, go out and walk directly there, as though following a compass, and find it.

He finds everything – if it is cold, a small stove and wood, hay and straw, a table and chairs – but above all food. It is uncanny; one would think he conjured it out of the air. His masterpiece was four

boxes of lobsters. Admittedly we would rather have had a good beef-
steak.

We have settled ourselves on the sunny side of the hut. There is a
smell of tar, of summer, and of sweaty feet. Kat sits beside me. He
wants to talk. To-day we have been practising saluting because Tjaden
failed to salute a major. Kat can't get it out of his head.

"You see, we are losing the war because we can salute too well,"
he says.

Kropp stalks up, with his breeches rolled up and his feet bare. He
lays out his washed socks to dry on the grass.

The two begin to argue. At the same time they lay a bottle of beer
on the result of an air-fight that's going on above us. Katczinsky won't
budge from the opinion, which as an old front-hog, he rhymes:

> Give 'em all the same grub and all the same pay
> And the war would be over and done in a day.

Kropp on the other hand is a thinker. He proposes that a decla-
ration of war should be a kind of popular festival with entrance-
tickets and bands, like a bullfight. Then in the arena the ministers
and generals of the two countries, dressed in bathing-drawers and
armed with clubs, can have it out among themselves. Whoever survives, his country wins. That would be much simpler and more just
than this arrangement, where the wrong people do the fighting.

The subject is dropped. Then the conversation turns to drill.

A picture comes before me. Burning midday in the barrack-yard.
The heat hangs over the square. The barracks are deserted. Everything sleeps. All one hears is the drummers practising; they have
installed themselves anywhere and practise brokenly, dully, monotonously. What a concord! Midday heat, barrack-square, and drummers beating!

The windows of the barracks are empty and dark. From some of them trousers are hanging to dry. The rooms are cool and one looks toward them longingly.

O dark, musty platoon huts, with the iron bedsteads, the chequered bedding, the lockers and the stools! Even you can become the object of desire; out here you have a faint resemblance to home; your rooms, full of the smell of stale food, sleep, smoke, and clothes!

Katczinsky paints it all in lively colours. What would we not give to be able to go back to it! But we must not pursue that line of thought any further.

Those early morning hours of instruction – "What are the parts of the 98 rifle?" – the midday hours of physical training – "Pianist, forward! By the right, quick march. Report to the cook-house for potato-peeling."

We indulge in reminiscences. Kropp laughs suddenly and says "Change at Löhne!"

That was our corporal's favourite game. Löhne is a railway junction. In order that our fellows going on leave shouldn't get lost there, Himmelstoss used to practise the change in the barrack-room. We had to learn that at Löhne, to reach the branch-line, we must pass through a subway. The beds represented the subway and each man stood at attention on the left side of his bed. Then came the command: "Change at Löhne!" and like lightning everyone scrambled under the bed to the opposite side. We practised this for a whole hour –

Meanwhile the German aeroplane has been shot down. Like a comet it bursts into a streamer of smoke and falls headlong. Kropp has lost the bottle of beer. Disgruntled he counts out the money from his wallet.

"Surely Himmelstoss was a very different fellow as a postman," say I, after Albert's disappointment has subsided. "Then how does it come that he's such a bully as a drill-sergeant?"

30

The question revives Kropp, more particularly as he hears there's no more beer in the canteen. "It's not only Himmelstoss, there are lots of them. As sure as they get a stripe or a star they become different men, just as though they'd swallowed concrete."

"That's the uniform," I suggest.

"Roughly speaking it is," says Kat, and prepares for a long speech; "but the root of the matter lies elsewhere. For instance, if you train a dog to eat potatoes and then afterwards put a piece of meat in front of him, he'll snap at it, it's his nature. And if you give a man a little bit of authority he behaves just the same way, he snaps at it too. The things are precisely the same. In himself man is essentially a beast, only he butters it over like a slice of bread with a little decorum. The army is based on that; one man must always have power over the other. The mischief is merely that each one has much too much power. A non-com. can torment a private, a lieutenant a non-com., a captain a lieutenant, until he goes mad. And because they know they can, they all soon acquire the habit more or less. Take a simple case: we are marching back from the parade-ground dog-tired. Then comes the order to sing. We are glad enough to be able to trail arms but we sing spiritlessly. At once the company is turned about and has to do another hour's drill as punishment. On the march back the order to sing is given again, and once more we start. Now what's the use of all that? It's simply that the company commander's head has been turned by having so much power. And nobody blames him. On the contrary, he is praised for being strict. That, of course, is only a trifling instance, but it holds also in very different affairs. Now I ask you: Let a man be whatever you like in peace time, what occupation is there in which he can behave like that without getting a crack on the nose? He can only do that in the army. It goes to the heads of them all, you see. And the more insignificant a man has been in civil life the worse it takes him."

"They say, of course, there must be discipline," ventures Kropp meditatively.

"True," growls Kat, "they always do. And it may be so; still it oughtn't to become an abuse. But you try to explain that to a black-smith or a labourer or a workman, you try to make that clear to a simple soldier – and that's what most of them are here. All he under-stands is that he has been properly trained so that when he comes up to the front he thinks he knows exactly what he should do in every circumstance and what not. It's simply amazing, I tell you, that the ordinary soldier survives so long up here in the front-line. Simply amazing!"

No one protests. Everyone knows that drill ceases only in the front-line and begins again a few miles behind, with all the absurdities of saluting and parade. It is an iron law that the soldier must be em-ployed under every circumstance.

Here Tjaden comes up with a flushed face. He is so excited that he stutters. Beaming with satisfaction he stammers out: "Himmelstoss is on his way. He's coming to the front!"

Tjaden has a special grudge against Himmelstoss, because of the way he educated him in the barracks. Tjaden wets his bed, he does it at night in his sleep. Himmelstoss maintained that it was sheer laziness and invented a method worthy of himself for curing Tjaden.

He hunted up another wet-a-bed, named Kindervater, from a neigh-bouring hut, and quartered him with Tjaden. In the huts there were the usual bunks, one above the other in pairs, with mattresses of wire netting. Himmelstoss put these two so that one occupied the upper and the other the lower bunk. The man underneath was of course disgusted. The next night they were changed over and the lower one put on top so that he could retaliate. That was Himmelstoss's system of self-education.

The idea was low but not ill-conceived. Unfortunately it accomplished nothing because the first assumption was wrong: it was not laziness in either of them. Anyone who looked at their sallow skin could see that. The matter ended in one of them always sleeping on the floor, where he frequently caught cold.

Meanwhile Haie sits down beside us. He winks at me and rubs his paws thoughtfully. We once spent the finest day of our army-life together – the day before we left for the front. We had been allotted to one of the recently formed regiments, but were first to be sent back for equipment to the garrison, not to the reinforcement-depot, of course, but to another barracks. We were due to leave next morning early. In the evening we prepared ourselves to square accounts with Himmelstoss.

We had sworn for weeks past to do this. Kropp had even gone so far as to propose entering the postal service in peace time in order to be Himmelstoss's superior when he became a postman again. He revelled in the thought of how he would grind him. It was this that made it impossible for him to crush us altogether – we always reckoned that later, at the end of the war, we would have our revenge on him.

In the meantime we decided to give him a good hiding. What could he do to us anyhow if he didn't recognize us and we left early the next morning?

We knew which pub he used to visit every evening. Returning to the barracks he had to go along a dark, uninhabited road. There we waited for him behind a pile of stones. I had a bed-cover with me. We trembled with suspense, hoping he would be alone. At last we heard his footstep, which we recognized easily, so often had we heard it in the mornings as the door flew open and he bawled: "Get up!"

"Alone?" whispered Kropp.

"Alone."

I slipped round the pile of stones with Tjaden.

Himmelstoss seemed a little elevated; he was singing. His belt-buckle gleamed. He came on unsuspectingly.

We seized the bed-cover, made a quick leap, threw it over his head from behind and pulled it round him so that he stood there in a white sack unable to raise his arms. The singing stopped. The next moment Haie Westhus was there, and spreading out his arms he shoved us back in order to be first in. He put himself in position with evident satisfaction, raised his arm like a signal-mast and his hand like a coal-shovel and fetched such a blow on the white sack as would have felled an ox.

Himmelstoss was thrown down, he rolled five yards and started to yell. But we were prepared for that and had brought a cushion. Haie squatted down, laid the cushion on his knees, felt where Himmelstoss's head was and pressed it down on the pillow. Immediately his voice was muffled. Haie let him get a gasp of air every so often, when he would give a mighty yell that was immediately hushed.

34

Tjaden unbuttoned Himmelstoss's braces and pulled down his trousers, holding the whip meantime in his teeth. Then he stood up and set to work.

It was a wonderful picture: Himmelstoss on the ground, Haie bending over him with a fiendish grin and his mouth open with bloodlust, Himmelstoss's head on his knees; then the convulsed, striped drawers, the crossed legs, executing at every blow most original movements in the lowered breeches, and towering over them like a woodcutter the indefatigable Tjaden. In the end we had to drag him away to get our turn.

Finally Haie stood Himmelstoss on his feet again and gave one last personal remonstrance. As he stretched out his right arm preparatory to giving him a box on the ear he looked as if he were going to reach down a star.

Himmelstoss staggered. Haie stood him up again, made ready and fetched him a second, well-aimed beauty with the left hand. Himmelstoss yelled and fell down on all fours cursing. His striped postman's backside gleamed in the moonlight.

We disappeared at full speed.

Haie looked round once again and said wrathfully, satisfied and rather mysteriously:

"Revenge is black-pudding."

Himmelstoss ought to have been pleased; his saying that we should each educate one another had borne fruit for himself. We had become successful students of his methods.

He never discovered whom he had to thank for the business. At any rate he scored a bed-cover out of it; for when we returned a few hours later to look for it, it was no longer to be found.

That evening's work made us more or less content to leave next morning. And an old buffer was pleased to describe us as "young heroes."

Chapter Four

WE HAVE TO go up on wiring fatigue. The motor lorries roll up after dark. We climb in. It is a warm evening and the twilight seems like a canopy under whose shelter we feel drawn together. Even the stingy Tjaden gives me a cigarette and then a light.

We stand jammed in together, shoulder to shoulder, there is no room to sit. But we do not expect that. Müller is in a good mood for once; he is wearing his new boots.

The engines drone, the lorries bump and rattle. The roads are worn and full of holes. We dare not show a light so we lurch along and are often almost pitched out. That does not worry us, however. It can happen if it likes; a broken arm is better than a hole in the guts, and many a man would be thankful enough for such a chance of finding his way home again.

Beside us stream the munition columns in long files. They are making the pace, they overtake us going forward. We joke with them and they answer back.

A wall becomes visible, it belongs to a house which lies on the side of the road. I suddenly prick up my ears. Am I deceived? Again I hear distinctly the cackle of geese. A glance at Katczinsky – a glance from him to me; we understand one another.

"Kat, I hear some aspirants for the frying-pan over there."

He nods. "It will be attended to when we come back. I have their number."

Of course Kat has their number. He knows all about every leg of goose within a radius of fifteen miles.

The lorries arrive at the artillery lines. The gun-emplacements are camouflaged with bushes against aerial observation, and look like a

36

kind of military Feast of the Tabernacles. These branches might seem gay and cheerful were not cannon embowered there.

The air becomes acrid with the smoke of the guns and the fog. The fumes of powder taste bitter on the tongue. The roar of the guns makes our lorry stagger, the reverberation rolls raging away to the rear, everything quakes. Our faces change imperceptibly. We are not, indeed, in the front-line, but only in the reserves, yet in every face can be read: This is the Front, now we are within its embrace.

It is not fear. Men who have been up as often as we have become thick skinned. Only the young recruits are agitated. Kat explains to them: "That was a twelve-inch. You hear the explosion first and afterwards comes the sound of the gun."

But the hollow sound of the firing does not reach us. It is swallowed up in the general murmur of the front. Kat listens: "There'll be a bombardment to-night."

We all listen. The front is restless. "The Tommies are firing already," says Kropp.

The shelling can be heard distinctly. It is the English batteries to the right of our section. They are beginning an hour too soon. According to us they start punctually at ten o'clock.

"What's got them?" says Müller, "their clocks must be fast."

"There'll be a bombardment, I tell you, I can feel it in my bones." Kat shrugs his shoulders.

Three shells land beside us. The burst of flame shoots across the fog, the fragments howl and drone. We shiver and are glad to think that we shall be back in the huts early in the morning.

Our faces are neither paler nor more flushed than usual; they are not more tense nor more flabby – and yet they are changed. We feel that in our blood a contact has shot home. That is no figure of speech; it is fact. It is the front, the consciousness of the front, that makes this contact. The moment that the first shells whistle over and the air is rent with the explosions, there is suddenly in our veins, in our hands, in our eyes, a tense waiting, a watching, a profound growth, a strange sharpening of the senses. The body with one bound is in full readiness.

It often seems to me as though it were the vibrating, shuddering air that with a noiseless leap springs upon us; or as though the front itself emitted an electric current which awakened unknown nerve-centres.

Every time it is the same. We start out for the front plain soldiers, either cheerful or gloomy; then come the first gun-emplacements and every word of our speech has a new ring.

When Kat stands in front of the hut and says: "There'll be a bombardment," that is merely his own opinion; but if he says it here, then the sentence has the sharpness of a bayonet in the moonlight, it cuts clean through the thought, it thrusts nearer and speaks to this unknown thing that is awakened in us, a dark meaning – "There'll be a bombardment." Perhaps it is our inner and most secret life that shivers and falls on guard.

To me the front is a mysterious whirlpool. Though I am in still water far away from its centre, I feel the whirl of the vortex sucking me slowly, irresistibly, inescapably into itself.

From the earth, from the air, sustaining forces pour into us – mostly from the earth. To no man does the earth mean so much as to the soldier. When he presses himself down upon her long and powerfully, when he buries his face and his limbs deep in her from the fear of death by shell-fire, then she is his only friend, his brother, his mother; he stifles his terror and his cries in her silence and her security; she shelters him and gives him a new lease of ten seconds of life, receives him again and often for ever.

Earth! – Earth! – Earth!

Earth with thy folds, and hollows and holes, into which a man may

38

fling himself and crouch down! In the spasm of terror, under the hailing of annihilation, in the bellowing death of the explosions, O Earth, thou grantest us the great resisting surge of new-won life. Our being, almost utterly carried away by the fury of the storm, streams back through our hands from thee, and we, thy redeemed ones, bury ourselves in thee, and through the long minutes in a mute agony of hope bite into thee with our lips!

At the sound of the first droning of the shells we rush back, in one part of our being, a thousand years. By the animal instinct that is awakened in us we are led and protected. It is not conscious; it is far quicker, much more sure, less fallible, than consciousness. One cannot explain it. A man is walking along without thought or heed; – suddenly he throws himself down on the ground and a storm of fragments flies harmlessly over him; – yet he cannot remember either to have heard the shell coming or to have thought of flinging himself down. But had he not abandoned himself to the impulse he would now be a heap of mangled flesh. It is this other, this second sight in us, that has thrown us to the ground and saved us, without our knowing how. If it were not so, there would not be one man alive from Flanders to the Vosges.

We march up, moody or good-tempered soldiers – we reach the zone where the front begins and become on the instant human animals.

An indigent-looking wood receives us. We pass by the soup-kitchens. Under cover of the wood we climb out. The lorries turn back. They are to collect us again in the morning, before dawn.

Mist and the smoke of guns lie breast-high over the fields. The moon is shining. Along the road troops file. Their helmets gleam softly in the moonlight. The heads and the rifles stand out above the white mist, nodding heads, rocking carriers of guns.

Farther on the mist ends. Here the heads become figures; coats, trousers, and boots appear out of the mist as from a milky pool. They become a column. The column marches on, straight ahead, the figures resolve themselves into a block, individuals are no longer recognizable, the dark wedge presses onward, fantastically topped by the heads and weapons floating off on the milky pool. A column – not men at all.

Guns and munition wagons are moving along a cross-road. The backs of the horses shine in the moonlight, their movements are beautiful, they toss their heads, and their eyes gleam. The guns and the wagons float before the dim background of the moonlit landscape, the riders in their steel helmets resemble knights of a forgotten time; it is strangely beautiful and arresting.

We push on to the pioneer dump. Some of us load our shoulders with pointed and twisted iron stakes; others thrust smooth iron rods through rolls of wire and go off with them. The burdens are awkward and heavy.

The ground becomes more broken. From ahead come warnings: "Look out, deep shell-holes on the left" – "Mind, trenches" –

Our eyes peer out, our feet and our sticks feel in front of us before they take the weight of the body. Suddenly the line halts; I bump my face against the roll of wire carried by the man in front and curse.

There are some shell-smashed lorries in the road. Another order: "Cigarettes and pipes out." We are getting near the line.

In the meantime it has become pitch dark. We skirt a small wood and then have the front-line immediately before us.

An uncertain, red glow spreads along the sky-line from one end to the other. It is in perpetual movement, punctuated with the bursts of flame from the muzzles of the batteries. Balls of light rise up high above it, silver and red spheres which explode and rain down in showers of red, white, and green stars. French rockets go up, which unfold a silk parachute to the air and drift slowly down. They light

40

up everything as bright as day, their light shines on us and we see our shadows sharply outlined on the ground. They hover for the space of a minute before they burn out. Immediately fresh ones shoot up to the sky, and again green, red, and blue stars.

"Bombardment," says Kat.

The thunder of the guns swells to a single heavy roar and then breaks up again into separate explosions. The dry bursts of the machine-guns rattle. Above us the air teems with invisible swift movement, with howls, pipings, and hisses. They are the smaller shells; – and amongst them, booming through the night like an organ, go the great coal-boxes and the heavies. They have a hoarse, distant bellow like a rutting stag and make their way high above the howl and whistle of the smaller shells. It reminds me of flocks of wild geese when I hear them. Last autumn the wild geese flew day after day across the path of the shells.

The searchlights begin to sweep the dark sky. They slide along it

41

like gigantic tapering rulers. One of them pauses, and quivers a little. Immediately a second is beside him, a black insect is caught between them and tries to escape – the airman. He hesitates, is blinded and falls.

At regular intervals we ram in the iron stakes. Two men hold a roll and the others spool off the barbed wire. It is that awful stuff with close-set, long spikes. I am not used to unrolling it and tear my hand.

After a few hours it is done. But there is still some time before the lorries come. Most of us lie down and sleep. I try also, but it has turned too chilly. Near to the sea one is constantly waked by the cold.

Once I fall fast asleep. Then waking suddenly with a start I do not know where I am. I see the stars, I see the rockets, and for a moment have the impression that I have fallen asleep at a garden fête. I don't know whether it is morning or evening, I lie in the pale cradle of the twilight, and listen for soft words which will come, soft and near – am I crying? I put my hand to my eyes, it is so fantastic; am I a child? Smooth skin; – it lasts only a second, then I recognize the silhouette of Katczinsky. The old veteran, he sits quietly and smokes his pipe – a covered pipe of course. When he sees I am awake, he says: "That gave you a fright. It was only a nose-cap, it landed in the bushes over there."

I sit up, I feel myself strangely alone. It's good Kat is there. He gazes thoughtfully at the front and says:

"Mighty fine fire-works if they weren't so dangerous."

One lands behind us. Two recruits jump up terrified. A couple of minutes later another comes over, nearer this time. Kat knocks out his pipe. "It makes a glow."

Then it begins in earnest. We crawl away as well as we can in our haste. The next lands fair among us. Two fellows cry out. Green rockets shoot up on the sky-line. Barrage. The mud flies high, fragments whizz past. The crack of the guns is heard long after the roar of the explosions.

42

Beside us lies a fair-headed recruit in utter terror. He has buried his face in his hands, his helmet has fallen off. I fish hold of it and try to put it back on his head. He looks up, pushes the helmet off and like a child creeps under my arm, his head close to my breast. The little shoulders heave. Shoulders just like Kemmerich's. I let him be. So that the helmet should be of some use I stick it on his behind; – not for a jest, but out of consideration, since that is his highest part. And though there is plenty of meat there, a shot in it can be damned painful. Besides, a man has to lie a whole month on his belly in the hospital, and afterwards he would be almost sure to have a limp.

It's got someone pretty badly. Cries are heard between the explosions.

At last it grows quiet. The fire has lifted over us and is now dropping on the reserves. We risk a look. Red rockets shoot up to the sky. Apparently there's an attack coming.

Where we are it is still quiet. I sit up and shake the recruit by the shoulder. "All over, kid! It's all right this time."

He looks round him dazedly. "You'll get used to it soon," I tell him.

He sees his helmet and puts it on. Gradually he comes to. Then suddenly he turns fiery red and looks confused. Cautiously he reaches his hand to his behind and looks at me dismally.

I understand at once: Gun-shy. That wasn't the reason I had stuck his helmet over it. "That's no disgrace," I reassure him: "Many's the man before you has had his pants full after the first bombardment. Go behind that bush there and throw your underpants away. Get along –"

He goes off. Things become quieter, but the cries do not cease. "What's up, Albert?" I ask.

"A couple of columns over there have got it in the neck."

The cries continue. It is not men, they could not cry so terribly.

"Wounded horses," says Kat.

43

It's unendurable. It is the moaning of the world, it is the martyred creation, wild with anguish, filled with terror, and groaning.

We are pale. Detering stands up. "God! For God's sake! Shoot them!"

He is a farmer and very fond of horses. It gets under his skin. Then as if deliberately the fire dies down again. The screaming of the beasts becomes louder. One can no longer distinguish whence in this now quiet, silvery landscape it comes; ghostly, invisible, it is everywhere, between heaven and earth it rolls on immeasurably. Detering raves and yells out: "Shoot them! Shoot them, can't you? damn you again!"

"They must look after the men first," says Kat quietly.

We stand up and try to see where it is. If we could only see the animals we should be able to endure it better. Müller has a pair of glasses. We see a dark group, bearers with stretchers, and larger black clumps moving about. Those are the wounded horses. But not all of them. Some gallop away in the distance, fall down, and then run on farther. The belly of one is ripped open, the guts trail out. He becomes tangled in them and falls, then he stands up again.

Detering raises his gun and aims. Kat hits it up in the air. "Are you mad – ?"

Detering trembles and throws his rifle on the ground.

We sit down and hold our ears. But this appalling noise, these groans and screams penetrate, they penetrate everywhere.

We can bear almost anything. But now the sweat breaks out on us. We must get up and run, no matter where, but where these cries can no longer be heard. And it is not men, only horses.

From the dark group stretchers move off again. Then single shots crack out. The black heap is convulsed and becomes thinner. At last! But still it is not the end. The men cannot overtake the wounded beasts which fly in their pain, their wide open mouths full of anguish. One of the men goes down on his knee, a shot – one horse drops – another. The last one props himself on his forelegs and drags himself round in a circle like a merry-go-round; squatting, it drags round in circles on its stiffened forelegs, apparently its back is broken. The soldier runs up and shoots it. Slowly, humbly it sinks to the ground.

We take our hands from our ears. The cries are silenced. Only a long-drawn, dying sigh still hangs on the air.

Then again only the rockets, the singing of the shells, and the stars — and they shine out wonderfully.

Detering walks up and down cursing: "Like to know what harm they've done." He returns to it once again. His voice is agitated, it sounds almost dignified as he says: "I tell you it is the vilest baseness to use horses in the war."

We go back. It is time we returned to the lorries. The sky is become a bit brighter. Three o'clock in the morning. The breeze is fresh and cool, the pale hour makes our faces look grey.

We trudge onward in single file through the trenches and shell-holes and come again to the zone of mist. Katczinsky is restive, that's a bad sign.

"What's up, Kat?" says Kropp.

"I wish I were back home." Home — he means the huts.

"It won't last much longer, Kat."

He is nervous. "I don't know, I don't know —"

We come to the communication-trench and then to the open fields. The little wood reappears; we know every foot of ground here. There's the cemetery with the mounds and the black crosses.

That moment it breaks out behind us, swells, roars, and thunders. We duck down — a cloud of flame shoots up a hundred yards ahead of us.

The next minute under a second explosion part of the wood rises slowly in the air, three or four trees sail up and then crash to pieces. The shells begin to hiss like safety-valves — heavy fire —

"Take cover!" yells somebody — "Cover!"

46

The fields are flat, the wood is too distant and dangerous – the only cover is the graveyard and the mounds. We stumble across in the dark and as though spirited away every man lies glued behind a mound.

Not a moment too soon. The dark goes mad. It heaves and raves. Darknesses blacker than the night rush on us with giant strides, over us and away. The flames of the explosions light up the graveyard.

There is no escape anywhere. By the light of the shells I try to get a view of the fields. They are a surging sea, daggers of flame from the explosions leap up like fountains. It is impossible for anyone to break through it.

The wood vanishes, it is pounded, crushed, torn to pieces. We must stay here in the graveyard.

The earth bursts before us. It rains clods. I feel a smack. My sleeve is torn away by a splinter. I shut my fist. No pain. Still that does not reassure me: wounds don't hurt till afterwards. I feel the arm all over. It is grazed but sound. Now a crack on the skull, I begin to lose consciousness. Like lightning the thought comes to me: Don't faint, sink down in the black broth and immediately come up to the top again. A splinter slashes into my helmet, but has travelled so far that it does not go through. I wipe the mud out of my eyes. A hole is torn up in front of me. Shells hardly ever land in the same hole twice, I'll get into it. With one bound I fling myself down and lie on the earth as flat as a fish; there it whistles again, quickly I crouch together, claw for cover, feel something on the left, shove in beside it, it gives way, I groan, the earth leaps, the blast thunders in my ears, I creep under the yielding thing, cover myself with it, draw it over me, it is wood, cloth, cover, cover, miserable cover against the whizzing splinters.

I open my eyes – my fingers grasp a sleeve, an arm. A wounded man? I yell to him – no answer – a dead man. My hand gropes farther, splinters of wood – now I remember again that we are lying in the graveyard.

47

But the shelling is stronger than everything. It wipes out the sensibilities, I merely crawl still deeper into the coffin, it should protect me, and especially as Death himself lies in it too.

Before me gapes the shell-hole. I grasp it with my eyes as with fists. With one leap I must be in it. There, I get a smack in the face, a hand clamps on to my shoulder — has the dead man waked up? — The hand shakes me, I turn my head, in the second of light I stare into the face of Katczinsky, he has his mouth wide open and is yelling. I hear nothing, he rattles me, comes nearer, in a momentary lull his voice reaches me: "Gas — Gaas — Gaaas — Pass it on."

I grab for my gas-mask. Some distance from me there lies someone. I think of nothing but this: That fellow there must know: Gaaas — Gaaas —

I call, I lean toward him, I swipe at him with the satchel, he doesn't see — once again, again — he merely ducks — it's a recruit — I look at Kat desperately, he has his mask ready — I pull out mine too, my helmet falls to one side, it slips over my face, I reach the man, his satchel is on the side nearest me, I seize the mask, pull it over his head, he understands, I let go and with a jump drop back into the shell-hole.

The dull thud of the gas-shells mingles with the crashes of the high explosives. A bell sounds between the explosions, gongs, and metal clappers warning everyone — Gas — Gas — Gaas.

Someone plumps down behind me, another. I wipe the goggles of my mask clear of the moist breath. It is Kat, Kropp, and someone else. All four of us lie there in a heavy, watchful suspense and breathe as lightly as possible.

48

These first minutes with the mask decide between life and death: is it tightly woven? I remember the awful sights in the hospital: the gas patients who in day-long suffocation cough their burnt lungs up in clots.

Cautiously, the mouth applied to the valve, I breathe. The gas still creeps over the ground and sinks into all hollows. Like a big, soft jelly-fish it floats into our shell-hole and lolls there obscenely. I nudge Kat, it is better to crawl out and lie on top than to stay here where the gas collects most. But we don't get as far as that; a second bombardment begins. It is no longer as though the shells roared; it is the earth itself raging.

With a crash something black bears down on us. It lands close beside us; a coffin thrown up.

I see Kat move and I crawl across. The coffin has hit the fourth man in our hole on his out-stretched arm. He tries to tear off his gas-mask with the other hand. Kropp seizes him just in time, twists the hand sharply behind his back and holds it fast.

Kat and I proceed to free the wounded arm. The coffin lid is loose and bursts open, we are easily able to pull it off, we toss the corpse out, it slides down to the bottom of the shell-hole, then we try to loosen the under-part.

Fortunately the man swoons and Kropp is able to help us. We no longer have to be careful, but work away till the coffin gives with a sigh before the spade that we have dug in under it.

It has grown lighter. Kat takes a piece of the lid, places it under the shattered arm, and we wrap all our bandages round it. For the moment we can do no more.

Inside the gas-mask my head booms and roars – it is nigh bursting. My lungs are tight, they breathe always the same hot, used-up air, the veins on my temples are swollen, I feel I am suffocating.

A grey light filters through to us. I climb out over the edge of the shell-hole. In the dirty twilight lies a leg torn clean off; the boot is quite whole, I take that all in at a glance. Now someone stands up a few yards distant. I polish the windows, in my excitement they are immediately dimmed again, I peer through them, the man there no longer wears his mask.

I wait some seconds – he has not collapsed – he looks around and makes a few paces – rattling in my throat I tear my mask off too and fall down, the air streams into me like cold water, my eyes are bursting, the wave sweeps over me and extinguishes me.

The shelling has ceased. I drag myself to the crater and tell the others. They take off their masks. We lift up the wounded man, one taking his splintered arm. And so we stumble off hastily.

The graveyard is a mass of wreckage. Coffins and corpses lie strewn about. They have been killed once again; but each of them that was flung up saved one of us.

The hedge is destroyed, the rails of the light railway are torn up and rise stiffly in the air in great arches. Someone lies in front of us. We stop; Kropp goes on alone with the wounded man.

50

The man on the ground is a recruit. His hip is covered with blood; he is so exhausted that I feel for my water-bottle where I have rum and tea. Kat restrains my hand and stoops over him.

"Where's it got you, comrade?"

His eyes move. He is too weak to answer.

We cut off his trousers carefully. He groans. "Gently, gently, it is much better –"

If he has been hit in the stomach he oughtn't to drink anything. There's no vomiting, that's a good sign. We lay the hip bare. It is one mass of mincemeat and bone splinters. The joint has been hit. This lad won't walk any more.

I wet his temples with a moistened finger and give him a swig. His eyes move again. We see now that the right arm is bleeding as well.

Kat spreads out two wads of dressing as wide as possible so that they will cover the wound. I look for something to bind loosely round it. We have nothing more, so I slit up the wounded man's trouser leg still farther in order to use a piece of his underpants as a bandage. But he is wearing none. I now look at him closely. He is the fair-headed boy of a little while ago.

In the meantime Kat has taken a bandage from a dead man's pocket and we carefully bind the wound. I say to the youngster who looks at us fixedly: "We're going for a stretcher now –"

Then he opens his mouth and whispers: "Stay here –"

"We'll be back again soon," said Kat. "We are only going to get a stretcher for you."

We don't know if he understands. He whimpers like a child and plucks at us: "Don't go away –"

Kat looks around and whispers: "Shouldn't we just take a revolver and put an end to it?"

The youngster will hardly survive the carrying, and at the most he will only last a few days. What he has gone through so far is nothing to what he's in for till he dies. Now he is numb and feels nothing. In an hour he will become one screaming bundle of intolerable pain. Every day that he can live will be a howling torture. And to whom does it matter whether he has them or not –

I nod. "Yes, Kat, we ought to put him out of his misery."

He stands still a moment. He has made up his mind. We look round – but we are no longer alone. A little group is gathering, from the shell-holes and trenches appear heads.

We get a stretcher.

Kat shakes his head. "Such a kid –" He repeats it: "Young innocents –"

Our losses are less than was to be expected – five killed and eight wounded. It was in fact quite a short bombardment. Two of our dead lie in the upturned graves. We had merely to throw the earth in on them.

We go back. We trot off silently in single file one behind the other. The wounded are taken to the dressing-station. The morning is cloudy. The bearers make a fuss about numbers and tickets, the wounded whimper. It begins to rain.

An hour later we reach our lorries and climb in. There is more room now than there was.

The rain becomes heavier. We take out waterproof sheets and spread them over our heads. The rain rattles down, and flows off at the sides in streams. The lorries bump through the holes, and we rock to and fro in a half-sleep.

Two men in the front of the lorry have long forked poles. They watch for telephone wires which hang crosswise over the road so densely that they might easily pull our heads off. The two fellows take them at the right moment on their poles and lift them over behind us. We hear their call: "Mind – wire –," dip the knee in a half-sleep and straighten up again.

52

Monotonously the lorries sway, monotonously come the calls, monotonously falls the rain. It falls on our heads and on the heads of the dead up in the line, on the body of the little recruit with the wound that is so much too big for his hip; it falls on Kemmerich's grave; it falls in our hearts.

An explosion sounds somewhere. We wince, our eyes become tense, our hands are ready to vault over the side of the lorry into the ditch by the road.

It goes no farther – only the monotonous cry: "Mind – wire" – our knees bend – we are again half asleep.

Chapter Five

KILLING each separate louse is a tedious business when a man has hundreds. The little beasts are hard and the everlasting cracking with one's fingernails very soon becomes wearisome. So Tjaden has rigged up the lid of a boot-polish tin with a piece of wire over the lighted stump of a candle. The lice are simply thrown into this little pan. Crack! and they're done for.

We sit around with our shirts on our knees, our bodies naked to the warm air and our hands at work. Haie has a particularly fine brand of louse: they have a red cross on their heads. He suggests that he brought them back with him from the hospital at Thourhout, where they attended personally on a surgeon-general. He says he means to use the fat that slowly accumulates in the tin-lid for polishing his boots, and roars with laughter for half an hour at his own joke.

But he hasn't much success to-day; we are too preoccupied with another affair.

The rumour has materialized. Himmelstoss has come. He appeared yesterday; we've already heard the well-known voice. He seems to have overdone it with a couple of young recruits on the ploughed field at home, and unknown to him the son of the local magistrate was watching. That cooked his goose.

He will meet some surprises here. Tjaden has been meditating for hours what to say to him. Haie gazes thoughtfully at his great paws and winks at me. The thrashing was the high-water mark of his life. He tells me he often dreams of it. Kropp and Müller are amusing themselves. From somewhere or other, probably the pioneer-cook-house, Kropp has bagged for himself a mess-tin full of beans. Müller squints hungrily into it but checks himself and says: "Albert, what would you do if it were suddenly peace time again?"

"There won't be any civil life," says Albert bluntly.

"Well, but if – " persists Müller, "what would you do?"

"Clear out of this!" growls Kropp.

"Of course. And then what?"

"Get drunk," says Albert.

54

"Don't talk rot, I mean seriously –"

"So do I," says Kropp, "what else should a man do?"

Kat becomes interested. He levies tribute on Kropp's tin of beans, swallows some, then considers for a while and says: "You might get drunk first, of course, but then you'd take the next train for home and mother. Peace time, man, Albert –"

He fumbles in his oil-cloth pocketbook for a photograph and suddenly shows it all round. "My old people!" Then he puts it back and swears: "Damned lousy war –"

"It's all very well for you to talk," I tell him. "You've a wife and children."

"True," he nods, "and I have to see to it that they've something to eat."

We laugh. "They won't lack for that, Kat, you'd scrounge it from somewhere."

Müller is insatiable and gives himself no peace. He wakes Haie Westhus out of his dream. "Haie, what would you do if it was peace time?"

"Give you a kick in the backside for the way you talk," I say. "How will it come about exactly?"

"How does the cow-dung come on the roof?" retorts Müller laconically, and turns to Haie Westhus again.

It is too much for Haie. He shakes his freckled head:

"You mean when the war's over?"

"Exactly. You've said it."

"Well, there'd be women of course, eh?" – Haie licks his lips.

"Sure."

"By Jove yes," says Haie, his face melting, "then I'd grab some good buxom dame, some real kitchen wench with plenty to get hold of, you know, and jump straight into bed. Just you think, boys, a real feather bed with a spring mattress; I wouldn't put trousers on again for a week."

55

Everyone is silent. The picture is too good. Our flesh creeps. At last Müller pulls himself together and says:

"And then what?"

A pause. Then Haie explains rather awkwardly: "If I were a non-com. I'd stay with the Prussians and serve out my time."

"Haie, you've got a screw loose, surely!" I say.

"Have you ever dug peat?" he retorts good-naturedly. "You try it."

Then he pulls a spoon out of the top of his boot and reaches over into Kropp's mess-tin.

"It can't be worse than digging trenches," I venture.

Haie chews and grins: "It lasts longer though. And there's no getting out of it either."

"But, man, surely it's better at home."

"Some ways," says he, and with open mouth sinks into a day-dream.

You can see what he is thinking. There is the mean little hut on the moors, the hard work on the heath from morning till night in the heat, the miserable pay, the dirty labourer's clothes.

"In the army in peace time you've nothing to trouble about," he goes on, "your food's found every day, or else you kick up a row; you've a bed, every week clean underwear like a perfect gent, you do your non-com.'s duty, you have a good suit of clothes; in the evening you're a free man and go off to the pub."

Haie is extraordinarily set on his idea. He's in love with it.

"And when your twelve years are up you get your pension and become a village bobby, and you can walk about the whole day."

He's already sweating on it. "And just you think how you'd be treated. Here a dram, there a pint. Everybody wants to be well in with a bobby."

"You'll never be a non-com. though, Haie," interrupts Kat.

Haie looks at him sadly and is silent. His thoughts still linger over the clear evenings in autumn, the Sundays in the heather, the village

56

bells, the afternoons and evenings with the servant girls, the fried bacon and barley, the care-free evening hours in the ale-house –

He can't part with all these dreams so abruptly; he merely growls: "What silly questions you do ask."

He pulls his shirt over his head and buttons up his tunic.

"What would you do, Tjaden?" asks Kropp.

Tjaden thinks only of one thing. "See to it that Himmelstoss doesn't get past me."

Apparently he would like most to have him in a cage and sail into him with a club every morning. To Kropp he says warmly: "If I were in your place I'd see to it that I became a lieutenant. Then you could grind him till the water in his backside boils."

"And you, Detering?" asks Müller like an inquisitor. He's a born schoolmaster with all his questions.

Detering is sparing with his words. But on this subject he speaks. He looks at the sky and says only the one sentence: "I would go straight on with the harvesting."

Then he gets up and walks off.

He is worried. His wife has to look after the farm. They've already taken away two of his horses. Every day he reads the papers that come, to see whether it is raining in his little corner of Oldenburg. They haven't brought the hay in yet.

At this moment Himmelstoss appears. He comes straight up to our group. Tjaden's face turns red. He stretches his length on the grass and shuts his eyes in embarrassment.

Himmelstoss is a little hesitant, his gait becomes slower. Then he marches up to us. No one makes any motion to stand up. Kropp looks up at him with interest.

He continues to stand in front of us and wait. As no one says anything he launches a "Well?"

A couple of seconds go by. Apparently Himmelstoss doesn't quite

57

know what to do. He would like most to set us all on the run again. But he seems to have learned already that the front-line isn't a parade-ground. He tries it on though, and by addressing himself to one instead of to all of us hopes to get some response. Kropp is nearest, so he favours him.

"Well, you here too?"

But Albert's no friend of his. "A bit longer than you, I fancy," he retorts.

The red moustache twitches: "You don't recognize me any more, what?"

Tjaden now opens his eyes. "I do though."

Himmelstoss turns to him: "Tjaden, isn't it?"

Tjaden lifts his head. "And do you know what you are?"

Himmelstoss is disconcerted. "Since when have we become so familiar? I don't remember that we ever slept in the gutter together?"

He has no idea what to make of the situation. He didn't expect this open hostility. But he is on his guard: someone has already dinned some rot into him about getting a shot in the back.

The question about the gutter makes Tjaden

so mad that he becomes almost witty: "No, you slept there by your-self."

Himmelstoss begins to boil. But Tjaden gets in ahead of him. He must bring off his insult: "Wouldn't you like to know what you are? A dirty hound, that's what you are. I've been wanting to tell you that for a long time."

The satisfaction of months shines in his dull pig's eyes as he spits out: "Dirty hound!"

Himmelstoss lets fly too, now. "What's that, you muck-rake, you dirty peat-stealer? Stand up there, bring your heels together when your superior officer speaks to you."

Tjaden winks solemnly. "You take a run and jump at yourself, Himmelstoss."

Himmelstoss is a raging book of army regulations. The Kaiser couldn't be more insulted. "Tjaden, I command you, as your superior officer: Stand up!"

"Anything else you would like?" asks Tjaden.

"Will you obey my order or not?"

Tjaden replies, without knowing it, in the well-known classical phrase.

At the same time he ventilates his backside.

"I'll have you court-martialled," storms Himmelstoss.

We watch him disappear in the direction of the Orderly Room. Haie and Tjaden burst into a regular peat-digger's bellow. Haie laughs so much that he dislocates his jaw, and suddenly stands there helpless with his mouth wide open. Albert has to put it back again by giving it a blow with his fist.

Kat is troubled: "If he reports you, it'll be pretty serious."

"Do you think he will?" asks Tjaden.

"Sure to," I say.

"The least you'll get will be five days close arrest," says Kat.

That doesn't worry Tjaden. "Five days clink are five days rest."

"And if they send you to the Fortress?" urges the thoroughgoing Müller.

"Well, for the time being the war will be over so far as I am concerned."

Tjaden is a cheerful soul. There aren't any worries for him. He goes off with Haie and Leer so that they won't find him in the first flush of the excitement.

Müller hasn't finished yet. He tackles Kropp again.

"Albert, if you were really at home now, what would you do?"

Kropp is contented now and more accommodating:

"How many of us were there in the class exactly?"

We count up: out of twenty, seven are dead, four wounded, one in a mad-house. That makes twelve privates.

"Three of them are lieutenants," says Müller. "Do you think they would still let Kantorek sit on them?"

We guess not: we wouldn't let ourselves be sat on for that matter.

"What do you mean by the three-fold theme in 'William Tell'?" says Kropp reminiscently, and roars with laughter.

"What was the purpose of the Poetic League of Göttingen?" asks Müller suddenly and earnestly.

"How many children had Charles the Bald?" I interrupt gently.

"You'll never make anything of your life, Bäumer," croaks Müller.

"When was the Battle of Zana?" Kropp wants to know.

"You lack the studious mind, Kropp, sit down, three minus — " I wink.

"What offices did Lycurgus consider the most important for the state?" asks Müller, pretending to take off his pince-nez.

"Does it go: 'We Germans fear God and none else in the whole world,' or 'We, the Germans, fear God and — ' " I submit.

"How many inhabitants has Melbourne?" asks Müller.

60

"How do you expect to succeed in life if you don't know that?" I ask Albert hotly.

Which he caps with: "What is meant by Cohesion?"

We remember mighty little of all that rubbish. Anyway, it has never been the slightest use to us. At school nobody ever taught us how to light a cigarette in a storm of rain, nor how a fire could be made with wet wood – nor that it is best to stick a bayonet in the belly because there it doesn't get jammed, as it does in the ribs.

Müller says thoughtfully: "What's the use? We'll have to go back and sit on the forms again."

I consider that out of the question. "We might take a special exam."

"That needs preparation. If you do get through, what then? A student's life isn't any better. If you have no money, you have to work like the devil."

"It's a bit better. But it's rot all the same, everything they teach you."

Kropp supports me: "How can a man take all that stuff seriously when he's once been out here?"

"Still you must have an occupation of some sort," insists Müller, as though he were Kantorek himself.

Albert cleans his nails with a knife. We are surprised at this delicacy. But it is merely pensiveness. He puts the knife away and continues: "That's just it. Kat and Detering and Haie will go back to their jobs because they had them already. Himmelstoss too. But we never had any. How will we ever get used to one after this, here?" – he makes a gesture toward the front.

"We'll want a private income, and then we'll be able to live by ourselves in a wood," I say, but at once feel ashamed of this absurd idea.

"But what will really happen when we go back?" wonders Müller, and even he is troubled.

Kropp gives a shrug. "I don't know. Let's get back first, then we'll find out."

We are all utterly at a loss. "What could we do?" I ask.

"I don't want to do anything," replies Kropp wearily. "You'll be dead one day, so what does it matter? I don't think we'll ever go back."

"When I think about it, Albert," I say after a while, rolling over on my back, "when I hear the word 'peacetime,' it goes to my head; and if it really came, I think I would do some unimaginable thing – something, you know, that it's worth having lain here in the muck for. But I can't even imagine anything. All I do know is that this business about professions and studies and salaries and so on – it makes me sick, it is and always was disgusting. I don't see anything – I don't see anything at all, Albert."

All at once everything seems to me confused and hopeless.

Kropp feels it too. "It will go pretty hard with us all. But nobody at home seems to worry much about it. Two years of shells and bombs – a man won't peel that off as easy as a sock."

We agree that it's the same for everyone; not only for us here, but everywhere, for everyone who is of our age; to some more, and to others less. It is the common fate of our generation.

Albert expresses it: "The war has ruined us for everything."

He is right. We are not youths any longer. We don't want to take the world by storm. We are fleeing. We fly from ourselves. From our life. We were eighteen and had begun to love life and the world; and we had to shoot it to pieces. The first bomb, the first explosion, burst in our hearts. We are cut off from activity, from striving, from progress. We believe in such things no longer, we believe in the war.

The Orderly Room shows signs of life. Himmelstoss seems to have stirred them up. At the head of the column trots the fat sergeant-major. It is queer that almost all pay-sergeant-majors are fat.

Himmelstoss follows him, thirsting for vengeance. His boots gleam in the sun.

We get up.

"Where's Tjaden?" the sergeant puffs.

No one knows, of course. Himmelstoss glowers at us wrathfully. "You know very well. You won't say, that's the fact of the matter. Out with it!"

Fatty looks round enquiringly; but Tjaden is not to be seen. He tries another way.

"Tjaden will report at the Orderly Room in ten minutes."

Then he steams off with Himmelstoss in his wake.

"I have a feeling that next time we go up wiring I'll be letting a bundle of wire fall on Himmelstoss's leg," hints Kropp.

"We'll have quite a lot of jokes with him," laughs Müller.

That is our sole ambition: to knock the conceit out of a postman.

I go into the hut and put Tjaden wise. He disappears.

Then we change our possy and lie down again to play cards. We know how to do that: to play cards, to swear, and to fight. Not much for twenty years; – and yet too much for twenty years.

Half an hour later Himmelstoss is back again. Nobody pays any attention to him. He asks for Tjaden. We shrug our shoulders.

"Then you'd better find him," he persists. "Haven't you been to look for him?"

Kropp lies back in the grass and says: "Have you ever been out here before?"

"That's none of your business," retorts Himmelstoss. "I expect an answer."

"Very good," says Kropp, getting up. "See up there where those little white clouds are. Those are anti-aircraft. We were over there yesterday. Five dead and eight wounded. It was a lot of fun. Next time, when you go up with us, before they die the fellows will come up to you, click their heels, and ask stiffly: 'Please may I go? Please may I hop it? We've been waiting here a long time for someone like you.' "

He sits down again and Himmelstoss disappears like a comet.

"Three days C.B.," Kat conjectures.

"Next time I'll let fly," I say to Albert.

But that is the end. The case comes up for trial in the evening. In the Orderly Room sits our Lieutenant, Bertinck, and calls us in one after another.

I have to appear as a witness and explain the reason of Tjaden's insubordination.

The story of the bed-wetting makes an impression. Himmelstoss is recalled and I repeat my statement.

"Is that right?" Bertinck asks Himmelstoss.

He tries to evade the question, but in the end has to confess, for Kropp tells the same story.

"Why didn't someone report the matter, then?" asks Bertinck.

We are silent: he must know himself how much use it is reporting such things in the army. It isn't usual to make complaints in the army. He understands it all right though, and lectures Himmelstoss, making it plain to him that the front isn't a parade-ground. Then comes Tjaden's turn, who gets a long sermon and three days' open arrest. He gives Kropp a wink and one day's open arrest. "It can't be helped," he says to him regretfully. He is a decent fellow.

Open arrest is quite pleasant. The clink was once a fowl-house; there we can visit the prisoners, we know how to manage it. Close arrest would have meant the cellar.

They used to tie us to a tree, but that is forbidden now. In many ways we are treated quite like men.

An hour after Tjaden and Kropp are settled in behind their wire netting we make our way in to them. Tjaden greets us crowing. Then we play skat far into the night. Tjaden wins of course, the lucky wretch.

When we break up Kat says to me: "What do you say to some roast goose?"

"Not bad," I agree.

We climb up on a munition-wagon. The ride costs us two cigarettes. Kat has marked the spot exactly. The shed belongs to a regimental headquarters. I agree to get the goose and receive my instructions. The out-house is behind the wall and the door shuts with just a peg.

Kat hoists me up. I rest my foot in his hands and climb over the wall. Kat keeps watch below.

I wait a few moments to accustom my eyes to the darkness. Then I recognize the shed. Softly I steal across, lift the peg, pull it out and open the door.

I distinguish two white patches. Two geese, that's bad: if I grab one the other will cackle. Well, both of them – if I'm quick, it can be done.

I make a jump. I catch hold of one and the next instant the second. Like a madman I bash their heads against the wall to stun them. But I haven't quite enough weight. The beasts cackle and strike out with their feet and wings. I fight desperately, but Lord! what a kick a goose has! They struggle and I stagger about. In the dark these white patches are terrifying. My arms have grown wings and I'm almost afraid of going up into the sky, as though I held a couple of captive balloons in my fists.

Then the row begins; one of them gets his breath and goes off like an alarm clock. Before I can do anything, something comes in from outside; I feel a blow, lie outstretched on the floor, and hear awful growls. A dog. I steal a glance to the side, he makes a snap at my throat. I lie still and tuck my chin into my collar.

It's a bull dog. After an eternity he withdraws his head and sits down beside me. But if I make the least movement he growls. I consider. The only thing to do is to get hold of my small revolver, and that too before anyone arrives. Inch by inch I move my hand toward it.

I have the feeling that it lasts an hour. The slightest movement and then an awful growl; I lie still, then try again. When at last I have the revolver my hand starts to tremble. I press it against the ground and then say over to myself: Jerk the revolver up, fire before he has a chance to grab, and then jump up.

Slowly I take a deep breath and become calmer. Then I hold my breath, whip up the revolver, it cracks, the dog leaps howling to one side, I make for the door of the shed and fall head over heels over one of the damned geese.

At full speed I seize it again, and with a swing toss it over the wall and clamber up. No sooner am I on top than the dog is up again as lively as ever and springs at me. Quickly I let myself drop. Ten paces away stands Kat with the goose under his arm. As soon as he sees me we run.

At last we can take a breather. The goose is dead, Kat saw to that in a moment. We intend to roast it, without telling anybody. I fetch a stove and wood from the hut and we crawl into a small deserted lean-to which we use for such purposes. The single window space is heavily curtained. There is a sort of hearth, an iron plate set on some bricks. We kindle a fire.

Kat plucks and cleans the goose. We put the feathers carefully to one side. We intend to make two cushions out of them with the in-scription: "Sleep soft under shell-fire." The sound of the gun-fire from the front penetrates into our refuge. The glow of the fire lights up our faces, shadows dance on the wall. Sometimes a heavy crash and the hut shivers. Aeroplane bombs. Once we hear a stifled cry. A hut must have been hit.

Aeroplanes drone; the tack-tack of machine-guns breaks out. But no light that could be observed shows from us.

66

We sit opposite one another, Kat and I, two soldiers in shabby coats, cooking a goose in the middle of the night. We don't talk much, but I believe we have a more complete communion with one another than even lovers have.

We are two men, two minute sparks of life; outside is the night and the circle of death. We sit on the edge of it crouching in danger, the grease drips from our hands, in our hearts we are close to one another, and the hour is like the room: flecked over with the lights and shadows of our feelings cast by a quiet fire. What does he know of me or I of him? Formerly we should not have had a single thought in common – now we sit with a goose between us and feel in unison, and are so intimate that we do not even speak.

It takes a long time to roast a goose, even when it is young and fat. So we take turns. One bastes it while the other lies down and sleeps. A grand smell gradually fills the hut.

The noises without increase in volume, pass into my dream and yet linger in my memory. In a half sleep I watch Kat dip and raise the ladle. I love him, his shoulders, his angular, stooping figure – and at the same time I see behind him woods and stars, and a clear voice utters words that bring me peace, to me, a soldier in big boots, belt, and knapsack, taking the road that lies before him under the high heaven, quickly forgetting and seldom sorrowful, for ever pressing on under the wide night sky.

A little soldier and a clear voice, and if anyone were to caress him he would hardly understand, this soldier with the big boots and shut heart, who marches because he is wearing big boots, and has forgotten all else but marching. Beyond the sky-line is a country with flowers, lying so still that he would like to weep. There are sights there that he has not forgotten, because he never possessed them – perplexing, yet lost to him. Are not his twenty summers there?

Is my face wet, and where am I? Kat stands before me, his gigantic, stooping shadow falls upon me like home. He speaks gently, he smiles and goes back to the fire.

Then he says: "It's done."

"Yes, Kat."

I stir myself. In the middle of the room shines the brown goose. We take out our collapsible forks and our pocket-knives and each cuts off a leg. With it we have army bread dipped in gravy. We eat slowly and with gusto.

"How does it taste, Kat?"

"Good! And yours?"

"Good, Kat."

We are brothers and press on one another the choicest pieces. Afterwards I smoke a cigarette and Kat a cigar. There is still a lot left.

"How would it be, Kat, if we took a bit to Kropp and Tjaden?"

"Sure," says he.

We carve off a portion and wrap it up carefully in newspaper. The rest we thought of taking over to the hut. Kat laughs, and simply says: "Tjaden."

I agree, we will have to take it all.

So we go off to the fowl-house to wake them. But first we pack away the feathers.

Kropp and Tjaden take us for magicians. Then they get busy with their teeth. Tjaden holds a wing in his mouth with both hands like a mouth-organ, and gnaws. He drinks the gravy from the pot and smacks his lips:

"May I never forget you!"

We go to our hut. Again there is the lofty sky with the stars and the oncoming dawn, and I pass on beneath it, a soldier with big boots and a full belly, a little soldier in the early morning – but by my side, stooping and angular, goes Kat, my comrade.

The outlines of the huts are upon us in the dawn like a dark, deep sleep.

Chapter Six

THERE ARE rumours of an offensive. We go up to the front two days earlier than usual. On the way we pass a shelled school-house. Stacked up against its longer side is a high double wall of yellow, un-polished, brand-new coffins. They still smell of fir, and pine, and the forest. There are at least a hundred.

"That's a good preparation for the offensive," says Müller astonished.

"They're for us," growls Detering.

"Don't talk rot," says Kat to him angrily.

"You be thankful if you get so much as a coffin," grins Tjaden, "they'll slip you a waterproof sheet for your old Aunt Sally of a carcase."

The others jest too, unpleasant jests, but what else can a man do? – The coffins are really for us. The organization surpasses itself in that kind of thing.

Ahead of us everything is simmering. The first night we try to get our bearings. When it is fairly quiet we can hear the transports behind the enemy lines rolling ceaselessly until dawn. Kat says they do not go back but are bringing up troops – troops, munitions, and shells.

The English artillery has been strengthened, that we can detect at once. There are at least four more batteries of twenty-fives to the right of the farm, and behind the poplars they have put in trench-mortars. Besides these they have brought up a number of those little French beasts with instantaneous fuses.

We are in low spirits. After we have been in the dug-outs two hours our own shells begin to fall in the trench. This is the third time in four weeks. If it were simply a mistake in aim no one would say anything, but the truth is that the barrels are worn out. The shots are often so uncertain that they land within our own lines. To-night two of our men were wounded by them.

The front is a cage in which we must await fearfully whatever may happen. We lie under the network of arching shells and live in a suspense of uncertainty. Over us Chance hovers. If a shot comes, we can duck, that is all; we neither know nor can determine where it will fall.

It is this Chance that makes us indifferent. A few months ago I was sitting in a dug-out playing skat; after a while I stood up and went to visit some friends in another dug-out. On my return nothing more was to be seen of the first one, it had been blown to pieces by a direct hit. I went back to the second and arrived just in time to lend a hand digging it out. In the interval it had been buried.

It is just as much a matter of chance that I am still alive as that I might have been hit. In a bomb-proof dug-out I may be smashed to atoms and in the open may survive ten hours' bombardment unscathed. No soldier outlives a thousand chances. But every soldier believes in Chance and trusts his luck.

70

We must look out for our bread. The rats have become much more numerous lately because the trenches are no longer in good condition. Detering says it is a sure sign of a coming bombardment.

The rats here are particularly repulsive, they are so fat – the kind we call corpse-rats. They have shocking, evil, naked faces, and it is nauseating to see their long, nude tails.

They seem to be mighty hungry. Almost every man has had his bread gnawed. Kropp wrapped his in his waterproof sheet and put it under his head, but he cannot sleep because they run over his face to get at it. Detering meant to outwit them: he fastened a thin wire to the roof and suspended his bread from it. During the night when he switched on his pocket-torch he saw the wire swinging to and fro. On the bread was riding a fat rat.

At last we put a stop to it. We cannot afford to throw the bread away, because already we have practically nothing left to eat in the morning, so we carefully cut off the bits of bread that the animals have gnawed.

The slices we cut off are heaped together in the middle of the floor. Each man takes out his spade and lies down prepared to strike. Detering, Kropp, and Kat hold their pocket-lamps ready.

After a few minutes we hear the first shuffling and tugging. It grows, now it is the sound of many little feet. Then the torches switch on and every man strikes at the heap, which scatters with a rush. The result is good. We toss the bits of rat over the parapet and again lie in wait.

Several times we repeat the process. At last the beasts get wise to it, or perhaps they have scented the blood. They return no more. Nevertheless, before morning the remainder of the bread on the floor has been carried off.

In the adjoining sector they attacked two large cats and a dog, bit them to death and devoured them.

Next day there is an issue of Edamer cheese. Each man gets almost a quarter of a cheese. In one way that is all to the good, for Edamer is tasty – but in another way it is vile, because the fat red balls have long been a sign of a bad time coming. Our forebodings increase as rum is served out. We drink it of course; but are not greatly comforted.

For days we loaf about and make war on the rats. Ammunition and hand-grenades become more plentiful. We even overhaul the bayonets – that is to say, the ones that have a saw on the blunt edge. If the fellows over there catch a man with one of those he's killed at sight. In the next sector some of our men were found whose noses were cut off and their eyes poked out with their own saw-bayonets. Their mouths and noses were stuffed with sawdust so that they suffocated.

Some of the recruits have bayonets of this kind; we take them away and give them the ordinary kind.

But the bayonet has practically lost its importance. It is usually the fashion now to charge with bombs and spades only. The sharpened spade is a more handy and many-sided weapon; not only can it be used for jabbing a man under the chin, but it is much better for striking with because of its greater weight; and if one hits between the neck and shoulder it easily cleaves as far down as the chest. The bayonet frequently jams on the thrust and then a man has to kick hard on the other fellow's belly to pull it out again; and in the interval he may easily get one himself. And what's more, the blade often gets broken off.

At night they send over gas. We expect the attack to follow and lie with our masks on, ready to tear them off as soon as the first shadow appears.

Dawn approaches without anything happening – only the everlasting, nerve-wracking roll behind the enemy lines, trains, trains, lorries, lorries; but what are they concentrating? Our artillery fires on it continually, but still it does not cease.

We have tired faces and avoid each other's eyes. "It will be like the Somme," says Kat gloomily. "There we were shelled steadily for seven days and nights." Kat has lost all his fun since we have been here, which is bad, for Kat is an old front-hog, and can smell what is coming. Only Tjaden seems pleased with the good rations and the rum; he thinks we might even go back to rest without anything happening at all.

It almost looks like it. Day after day passes. At night I squat in the listening-post. Above me the rockets and parachute-lights shoot up and float down again. I am cautious and tense, my heart thumps. My eyes turn again and again to the luminous dial of my watch; the hands will not budge. Sleep hangs on my eyelids, I work my toes in my boots in order to keep awake. Nothing happens till I am relieved; – only the everlasting rolling over there. Gradually we grow calmer and play skat and poker continually. Perhaps we will be lucky.

All day the sky is hung with observation balloons. There is a rumour that the enemy are going to put tanks over and use low-flying planes for the attack. But that interests us less than what we hear of the new flame-throwers.

We wake up in the middle of the night. The earth booms. Heavy fire is falling on us. We crouch into corners. We distinguish shells of every calibre.

Each man lays hold of his things and looks again every minute to reassure himself that they are still there. The dug-out heaves, the night roars and flashes. We look at each other in the momentary flashes of light, and with pale faces and pressed lips shake our heads.

Every man is aware of the heavy shells tearing down the parapet, rooting up the embankment and demolishing the upper layers of concrete. When a shell lands in the trench we note how the hollow, furious blast is like a blow from the paw of a raging beast of prey. Already by morning a few of the recruits are green and vomiting. They are too inexperienced.

Slowly the grey light trickles into the post and pales the flashes of the shells. Morning is come. The explosion of mines mingles with the gun-fire. That is the most dementing convulsion of all. The whole region where they go up becomes one grave.

The reliefs go out, the observers stagger in, covered with dirt, and trembling. One lies down in silence in the corner and eats, the other, a reservist-reinforcement, sobs; twice he has been flung over the parapet by the blast of explosions without getting any more than shell-shock.

The recruits are eyeing him. We must watch them, these things are catching, already some lips begin to quiver. It is good that it is growing daylight; perhaps the attack will come before noon.

The bombardment does not diminish. It is falling in the rear too.

74

As far as one can see it spouts fountains of mud and iron. A wide belt is being raked.

The attack does not come, but the bombardment continues. Slowly we become mute. Hardly a man speaks. We cannot make ourselves understood.

Our trench is almost gone. At many places it is only eighteen inches high, it is broken by holes, and craters, and mountains of earth. A shell lands square in front of our post. At once it is dark. We are buried and must dig ourselves out. After an hour the entrance is clear again, and we are calmer because we have had something to do.

Our company commander scrambles in and reports that two dugouts are gone. The recruits calm themselves when they see him. He says that an attempt will be made to bring up food this evening.

This sounds reassuring. No one had thought of it except Tjaden. Now the outside world seems to draw a little nearer: if food can be brought up, think the recruits, then it can't really be so bad.

We do not disabuse them; we know that food is as important as ammunition and only for that reason must be brought up.

But it miscarries. A second party goes out, and it also turns back. Finally Kat tries, and even he reappears without accomplishing anything. No one gets through, not even a fly is small enough to get through such a barrage.

We pull in our belts tighter and chew every mouthful three times as long. Still the food does not last out; we are damnably hungry. I take out a scrap of bread, eat the white and put the crust back in my knapsack; from time to time I nibble at it.

The night is unbearable. We cannot sleep, but stare ahead of us and doze. Tjaden regrets that we wasted the gnawed pieces of bread on the rats. We would gladly have them again to eat now. We are short of water, too, but not seriously yet.

75

Towards morning, while it is still dark, there is some excitement. Through the entrance rushes in a swarm of fleeing rats that try to storm the walls. Torches light up the confusion. Everyone yells and curses and slaughters. The madness and despair of many hours unloads itself in this outburst. Faces are distorted, arms strike out, the beasts scream; we just stop in time to avoid attacking one another.

The onslaught has exhausted us. We lie down to wait again. It is a marvel that our post has had no casualties so far. It is one of the few deep dug-outs.

A corporal creeps in; he has a loaf of bread with him. Three people have had the luck to get through during the night and bring some provisions. They say the bombardment extends undiminished as far as the artillery lines. It is a mystery where the enemy gets all his shells.

We wait and wait. By midday what I expected happens. One of the recruits has a fit. I have been watching him for a long time, grinding his teeth and opening and shutting his fists. These hunted, protruding eyes, we know them too well. During the last few hours he has had merely the appearance of calm. He had collapsed like a rotten tree.

Now he stands up, stealthily creeps across the floor, hesitates a moment and then glides towards the door. I intercept him and say: "Where are you going?"

"I'll be back in a minute," says he, and tries to push past me.

"Wait a bit, the shelling will stop soon."

He listens and for a moment his eye becomes clear. Then again he has the glowering eyes of a mad dog, he is silent, he shoves me aside.

"One minute, lad," I say. Kat notices. Just as the recruit shakes me off Kat jumps in and we hold him.

Then he begins to rave: "Leave me alone, let me go out, I will go out!"

He won't listen to anything and hits out, his mouth is wet and pours

76

out words, half-choked, meaningless words. It is a case of claustro-phobia, he feels as though he is suffocating here and wants to get out at any price. If we let him go he would run about everywhere regard-less of cover. He is not the first.

Though he raves and his eyes roll, it can't be helped, and we have to give him a hiding to bring him to his senses. We do it quickly and mercilessly, and at last he sits down quietly. The others have turned pale; let's hope it deters them. This bombardment is too much for the poor devils, they have been sent straight from a recruiting-depot into a barrage that is enough to turn an old soldier's hair grey.

After this affair the sticky, close atmosphere works more than ever on our nerves. We sit as if in our graves waiting only to be closed in.

Suddenly it howls and flashes terrifically, the dug-out cracks in all its joints under a direct hit, fortunately only a light one that the con-crete blocks are able to withstand. It rings metallically, the walls reel, rifles, helmets, earth, mud, and dust fly everywhere. Sulphur fumes pour in.

If we were in one of those light dug-outs that they have been build-ing lately instead of this deep one, not one of us would now be alive.

But the effect is bad enough even so. The recruit starts to rave again and two others follow suit. One jumps up and rushes out, we have trouble with the other two. I start after the one who escapes and wonder whether to shoot him in the leg – then it shrieks again, I fling myself down and when I stand up the wall of the trench is plastered with smoking splinters, lumps of flesh, and bits of uniform. I scramble back.

The first recruit seems actually to have gone insane. He butts his head against the wall like a goat. We must try to-night to take him to the rear. Meanwhile we bind him, but in such a way that in case of attack he can be released at once.

Kat suggests a game of skat: it is easier when a man has something to do. But it is no use, we listen for every explosion that comes close, miscount the tricks, and fail to follow suit. We have to give it up. We sit as though in a hissing boiler that is being belaboured from without on all sides.

Night again. We are deadened by the strain – a deadly tension that scrapes along one's spine like a gapped knife. Our legs refuse to move, our hands tremble, our bodies are a thin skin stretched painfully over repressed madness, over an almost irresistible, bursting roar. We have neither flesh nor muscles any longer, we dare not look at one another for fear of some incalculable thing. So we shut our teeth – it will end – it will end – perhaps we will come through.

Suddenly the nearer explosions cease. The shelling continues but it has lifted and falls behind us, our trench is free. We seize the hand-grenades, pitch them out in front of the dug-out and jump after them. The bombardment has stopped and a heavy barrage now falls behind us. The attack has come.

No one would believe that in this howling waste there could still be men; but steel helmets now appear on all sides out of the trench, and fifty yards from us a machine-gun is already in position and barking.

The wire entanglements are torn to pieces. Yet they offer some obstacle. We see the storm-troops coming. Our artillery opens fire. Ma-

78

chine-guns rattle, rifles crack. The charge works its way across. Haie and Kropp begin with the hand-grenades. They throw as fast as they can, others pass them, the handles with the strings already pulled. Haie throws seventy-five yards, Kropp sixty, it has been measured, the distance is important. The enemy as they run cannot do much before they are within forty yards.

We recognize the distorted faces, the smooth helmets: they are French. They have already suffered heavily when they reach the remnants of the barbed-wire entanglements. A whole line has gone down before our machine-guns; then we have a lot of stoppages and they come nearer.

I see one of them, his face upturned, fall into a wire cradle. His body collapses, his hands remain suspended as though he were praying. Then his body drops clean away and only his hands with the stumps of his arms, shot off, now hang in the wire.

The moment we are about to retreat three faces rise up from the ground in front of us. Under one of the helmets a dark pointed beard and two eyes that are fastened on me. I raise my hand, but I cannot throw into those strange eyes; for one mad moment the whole slaughter whirls like a circus round me, and these two eyes that are alone motionless; then the head rises up, a hand, a movement, and my hand-grenade flies through the air and into him.

We make for the rear, pull wire cradles into the trench and leave bombs behind us with the string pulled, which ensure us a fiery retreat. The machine-guns are already firing from the next position.

We have become wild beasts. We do not fight, we defend ourselves against annihilation. It is not against men that we fling our bombs, what do we know of men in this moment when Death with hands and helmets is hunting us down – now, for the first time in three days we can see his face, now, for the first time in three days we can oppose him; we feel a mad anger. No longer do we lie helpless, waiting on the scaffold, we can destroy and kill, to save ourselves, to save ourselves and be revenged.

We crouch behind every corner, behind every barrier of barbed wire, and hurl heaps of explosives at the feet of the advancing enemy before we run. The blast of the hand-grenades impinges powerfully on our arms and legs; crouching like cats we run on, overwhelmed by this wave that bears us along, that fills us with ferocity, turning us into thugs, into murderers, into God only knows what devils; this wave that multiplies our strength with fear and madness and greed of life, seeking and fighting for nothing but our deliverance. If your own father came over with them you would not hesitate to fling a bomb into him.

The forward trenches have been abandoned. Are they still trenches? They are blown to pieces, annihilated – there are only broken bits of trenches, holes linked by tracks, nests of craters, that is all. But the enemy's casualties increase. They did not count on so much resistance.

It is nearly noon. The sun blazes hotly, the sweat stings in our eyes, we wipe it off on our sleeves, and often blood with it. At last we reach a trench that is in a somewhat better condition. It is manned and ready

80

for the counter-attack, it receives us. Our guns open up in full blast and cut off the enemy attack.

The lines behind us stop. They can advance no farther. The attack is crushed by our artillery. We watch. The fire lifts a hundred yards and we break forward. Beside me a lance-corporal has his head torn off. He runs a few steps more while the blood spouts from his neck like a fountain.

It does not come quite to hand-to-hand fighting; they are driven back. We arrive once again at our shattered trench and pass on beyond it.

Oh, this turning back again! We reach the shelter of the reserves and yearn to creep in and disappear; – but instead we must turn round and plunge again into the horror. If we were not automata at that moment we would continue lying there, exhausted, and without will. But we are swept forward again, powerless, madly savage and raging; we will kill, for they are still our mortal enemies; their rifles and bombs are aimed against us, and if we don't destroy them, they will destroy us.

The brown earth, the torn, blasted earth, with a greasy shine under the sun's rays; the earth is the background of this restless, gloomy world of automatons, our gasping is the scratching of a quill, our lips are dry, our heads are debauched with stupor – thus we stagger forward, and into our pierced and shattered souls bores the torturing image of the brown earth with the greasy sun and the convulsed and dead soldiers, who lie there – it can't be helped – who cry and clutch at our legs as we spring away over them.

We have lost all feeling for one another. We can hardly control ourselves when our hunted glance lights on the form of some other man. We are insensible, dead men, who through some trick, some dreadful magic, are still able to run and to kill.

A young Frenchman lags behind, he is overtaken, he puts up his hands, in one he still holds his revolver – does he mean to shoot or to give himself up? – a blow from a spade cleaves through his face. A

second sees it and tries to run farther; a bayonet jabs into his back.
He leaps in the air, his arms thrown wide, his mouth wide open, yelling; he staggers, in his back the bayonet quivers. A third throws away
his rifle, cowers down with his hands before his eyes. He is left behind with a few other prisoners to carry off the wounded.

Suddenly in the pursuit we reach the enemy line.

We are so close on the heels of our retreating enemies that we reach
it almost at the same time as they. In this way we suffer few casualties.

82

A machine-gun barks, but is silenced with a bomb. Nevertheless, the couple of seconds has sufficed to give us five stomach wounds. With the butt of his rifle Kat smashes to pulp the face of one of the unwounded machine-gunners. We bayonet the others before they have time to get out their bombs. Then thirstily we drink the water they have for cooling the gun.

Everywhere wire-cutters are snapping, planks are thrown across the entanglements, we jump through the narrow entrances into the trenches. Haie strikes his spade into the neck of a gigantic Frenchman and throws the first hand-grenade; we duck behind a breastwork for a few seconds, then the whole section of trench before us is empty. The next throw whizzes obliquely over the corner and clears a passage; as we run past we toss handfuls down into the dug-outs, the earth shudders, it crashes; dully and stifled, we stumble over slippery lumps of flesh, over yielding bodies; I fall into an open belly on which lies a clean, new officer's cap.

The fight ceases. We lose touch with the enemy. We cannot stay here long but must retire under cover of our artillery to our own position. No sooner do we know this than we dive into the nearest dug-outs, and with the utmost haste seize on whatever provisions we can see, especially the tins of corned beef and butter, before we clear out.

We get back pretty well. There has been no further attack by the enemy. We lie for an hour panting and resting before anyone speaks. We are so completely played out that in spite of our great hunger we do not think of the provisions. Then gradually we become something like men again.

The corned beef over there is famous along the whole front. Occasionally it has been the chief reason for a flying raid on our part, for our nourishment is generally bad; we have a constant hunger.

We bagged five tins altogether. The fellows over there are well looked after; it seems a luxury to us with our hunger-pangs, our turnip jam, and meat so scarce that we simply grab at it. Haie has scored a thin loaf of white French bread, and stuck it in behind his belt like a spade. It is a bit bloody at one corner, but that can be cut off.

It is a good thing we have something decent to eat at last; we still have a use for all our strength. Enough to eat is just as valuable as a good dug-out; it can save our lives; that is the reason we are so greedy for it.

Tjaden has captured two water-bottles full of cognac. We pass them round.

The evening benediction begins. Night comes, out of the craters rise the mists. It looks as though the holes were full of ghostly secrets. The white vapour creeps painfully round before it ventures to steal away over the edge. Then long streaks stretch from crater to crater.

It is chilly. I am on sentry and stare into the darkness. My strength is exhausted as always after an attack, and so it is hard for me to be alone with my thoughts. They are not properly thoughts; they are memories which in my weakness turn homeward and strangely move me.

The parachute-lights shoot upwards – and I see a picture, a summer evening, I am in the cathedral cloister and look at the tall rose trees that bloom in the middle of the little cloister garden where the monks lie buried. Around the walls are the stone carvings of the Stations of the Cross. No one is there. A great quietness rules in this blossoming quadrangle, the sun lies warm on the heavy grey stones, I place my hand upon them and feel the warmth. At the right-hand corner the green cathedral spire ascends into the pale blue sky of the evening. Between the glowing columns of the cloister is the cool darkness that only churches have, and I stand there and wonder whether, when I am twenty, I shall have experienced the bewildering emotions of love.

The image is alarmingly near; it touches me before it dissolves in the light of the next star-shell.

I lay hold of my rifle to see that it is in trim. The barrel is wet, I take it in my hand and rub off the moisture with my fingers.

Between the meadows behind our town there stands a line of old poplars by a stream. They were visible from a great distance, and although they grew on one bank only, we called them the poplar avenue. Even as children we had a great love for them, they drew us vaguely thither, we played truant the whole day by them and listened to their rustling. We sat beneath them on the bank of the stream and let our feet hang over in the bright, swift waters. The pure fragrance of the water and the melody of the wind in the poplars held our fancies. We loved them dearly, and the image of those days still makes my heart pause in its beating.

It is strange that all the memories that come have these two qualities. They are always completely calm, that is predominant in them; and even if they are not really calm, they become so. They are soundless apparitions that speak to me, with looks and gestures, silently, without any word – and it is the alarm of their silence that forces me to lay hold of my sleeve and my rifle lest I should abandon myself to the liberation and allurement in which my body would dilate and gently pass away into the still forces that lie behind these things.

They are quiet in this way, because quietness is so unattainable for us now. At the front there is no quietness and the curse of the front reaches so far that we never pass beyond it. Even in the remote depots and rest-areas the droning and the muffled noise of shelling is always in our ears. We are never so far off that it is no more to be heard. But these last few days it has been unbearable.

Their stillness is the reason why these memories of former times do not awaken desire so much as sorrow – a strange, inapprehensible melancholy. Once we had such desires – but they return not. They are past, they belong to another world that is gone from us. In the barracks they called forth a rebellious, wild craving for their return; for then they were still bound to us, we belonged to them and they to us, even though we were already absent from them. They appeared in the soldiers' songs which we sang as we marched between the glow of the dawn and the black silhouettes of the forests to drill on the moor, they were a powerful remembrance that was in us and came from us.

But here in the trenches they are completely lost to us. They arise no more; we are dead and they stand remote on the horizon, they are an apparition, a mysterious reflection drawing us home, that we fear and love without hope. They are strong and our desire is strong — but they are unattainable, and we know it.

And even if these scenes of our youth were given back to us we would hardly know what to do. The tender, secret influence that passed from them into us could not arise again. We long to be in them and to move in them; we long to remember and to love them and to be stirred by the sight of them. But it would be like gazing at the photograph of a dead comrade; those are his features, it is his face, and the days we spent together take on a mournful life in the memory; but the man himself it is not.

We could never again, as the same beings, take part in those scenes. It was not any recognition of their beauty and their significance that attracted us, but the communion, the feeling of a comradeship with the things and events of our existence, which cut us off and made the world of our parents a thing incomprehensible to us — for then we surrendered ourselves to events and were lost in them, and the least little thing was enough to carry us down the stream of eternity. Perhaps it was only the privilege of our youth, but as yet we recognized no limits and saw nowhere an end. We had that thrill of expectation in the blood which united us with the course of our days.

To-day we would pass through the scenes of our youth like travellers. We are burnt up by hard facts; like tradesmen we understand distinctions, and like butchers, necessities. We are no longer untroubled — we are indifferent. We long to be there; but could we live there?

We are forlorn like children, and experienced like old men, we are crude and sorrowful and superficial — I believe we are lost.

My hands grow cold and my flesh creeps; and yet the night is warm. Only the mist is cold, this mysterious mist that trails the dead before us and sucks from them their last, creeping life. By morning they will be pale and green and their blood congealed and black.

Still the parachute-rockets shoot up and cast their pitiless light over the stony landscape, which is full of craters and frozen lights like a moon. The blood beneath my skin brings fear and restlessness into my thoughts. They become feeble and tremble, they desire warmth and life. They cannot endure without sympathy and communion, they are disordered before the naked picture of despair.

I hear the rattle of the mess-tins and immediately feel a strong desire for warm food; it would do me good and comfort me. Painfully I force myself to wait until I am relieved.

Then I go into the dug-out and find a mug of barley. It is cooked in fat and tastes good, I eat it slowly. I remain quiet, though the others are in a better mood, for the shelling has died down.

The days go by and the incredible hours follow one another as a matter of course. Attacks alternate with counter-attacks and slowly the dead pile up in the field of craters between the trenches. We are able to bring in most of the wounded that do not lie too far off. But many have long to wait and we listen to them dying.

For one of them we search two days in vain. He must be lying on his belly and unable to turn over. Otherwise it is hard to understand why we cannot find him; for it is only when a man has his mouth close to the ground that it is impossible to gauge the direction of his cry.

He must have been badly hit – one of those nasty wounds, neither so severe that they exhaust the body at once and a man dreams on in a half-swoon, nor so light that a man endures the pain in the hope of becoming well again. Kat thinks he has either a broken pelvis or a shot through the spine. His chest cannot have been injured, otherwise he would not have such strength to cry out. And if it were any other kind of wound it would be possible to see him moving.

100

He grows gradually hoarser. The voice sounds so desperate that it prevails everywhere. The first night some of our fellows go out three times to look for him. But when they think they have located him and crawl across, next time they hear the voice it seems to come from somewhere else altogether.

We search in vain until dawn. We scrutinize the field all day with glasses, but discover nothing. On the second day the calls are fainter; that will be because his lips and mouth have become dry.

Our company commander has promised special leave with three days extra to anyone who finds him. That is a powerful inducement, but we would do all that is possible without that; for his cry is terrible. Kat and Kropp even go out in the afternoon, and Albert gets the lobe of his ear shot off in consequence. It is to no purpose, they come back without him.

It is easy to understand what he cries. At first he called only for help – the second night he must have some delirium, he talks with his wife and his children, we often detect the name Elise. To-day he merely weeps. By evening the voice dwindles to a croaking. But it persists still through the whole night. We hear it so distinctly because the wind blows toward our line. In the morning when we suppose he must already have long gone to his rest, there comes across to us one last gurgling rattle.

The days are hot and the dead lie unburied. We cannot fetch them all in, if we did we should not know what to do with them. The shells will bury them. Many have their bellies swollen up like balloons. They hiss, belch, and make movements. The gases in them make noises.

The sky is blue and without clouds. In the evening it grows sultry and the heat rises from the earth. When the wind blows toward us it brings the smell of blood, which is heavy and sweet. This deathly exhalation from the shell-holes seems to be a mixture of chloroform and putrefaction, and fills us with nausea and retching.

The nights become quiet and the hunt for copper driving-bands and the silken parachutes of the French star-shells begins. Why the driving-bands are so desirable no one knows exactly. The collectors merely assert that they are valuable. Some have collected so many that they will stoop under the weight of them when we go back.

But Haie at least gives a reason. He intends to give them to his girl to supplement her garters. At this the Frisians explode with mirth. They slap their knees: "By Jove though, he's a wit, Haie is, he's got brains." Tjaden especially can hardly contain himself; he takes the largest of the rings in his hand and every now and then puts his leg through it to show how much slack there is.

"Haie, man, she must have legs like, legs – " his thoughts mount somewhat higher, "and a behind too she must have, like a – like an elephant!"

Haie beams, proud that his girl should receive so much appreciation.

"She's a nice bit," he says with self-satisfaction.

The parachutes are turned to more practical uses. According to the size of the bust three or perhaps four will make a blouse. Kropp and I use them as handkerchiefs. The others send them home. If the women could see at what risk these bits of rag are often obtained, they would be horrified.

Kat surprises Tjaden endeavouring with perfect equanimity to knock the driving-band off a dud. If anyone else had tried it the thing would have exploded, but Tjaden always has his luck with him.

One morning two butterflies play in front of our trench. They are brimstone-butterflies, with red spots on their yellow wings. What can they be looking for here? There is not a plant nor a flower for miles. They settle on the teeth of a skull. The birds too are just as carefree, they have long since accustomed themselves to the war. Every morning larks ascend from No Man's Land. A year ago we watched them nesting; the young ones grew up too.

We have a spell without rats in the trench. They are in No Man's Land – we know what for. They grow fat; when we see one we have a crack at it. At night we hear again the rolling behind the enemy lines. All day we have only the normal shelling, so that we are able to repair the trenches. There is always plenty of amusement, the airmen see to that. There are countless fights for us to watch every day.

Battle planes don't trouble us, but the observation planes we hate like the plague; they put the artillery on to us. A couple of minutes after they appear, shrapnel and high-explosives begin to drop on us. We lose eleven men in one day that way, and five of them stretcher-bearers. Two are so smashed that Tjaden remarks you could scrape them off the wall of the trench with a spoon and bury them in a mess-tin. Another has the lower part of his body and his legs torn off. Dead, his chest leans against the side of the trench, his face is lemon-yellow, in his beard still burns a cigarette. It glows until it dies out on his lips.

We put the dead in a large shell-hole. So far there are three layers, one on top of the other.

Suddenly the shelling begins to pound again. Soon we are sitting up once more with the rigid tenseness of blank anticipation.

Attack, counter-attack, charge, repulse – these are words, but what things they signify! We have lost a good many men, mostly recruits. Reinforcements have again been sent up to our sector. It is one of the new regiments, composed of young fellows called up during last year. They have had hardly any training, and are sent into the field with only a theoretical knowledge. They do know what a hand-grenade is, it is true, but they have very little idea of cover, and what is most important of all, have no eye for it. A fold in the ground has to be quite eighteen inches high before they can see it.

Although we need reinforcement, the recruits give us almost more trouble than they are worth. They are helpless in this grim fighting area, they fall like flies. The present method of fighting from posts demands knowledge and experience; a man must have a feeling for the contours of the ground, an ear for the sound and character of the shells, must be able to decide beforehand where they will drop, how they will burst, and how to shelter from them.

The young recruits of course know none of these things. They get killed simply because they can hardly tell shrapnel from high-explosive, they are mown down because they are listening anxiously to the roar of the big coal-boxes falling far in the rear, and miss the light, piping whistle of the low spreading little daisy-cutters. They flock together like sheep instead of scattering, and even the wounded are shot down like hares by the airmen.

Their pale turnip faces, their pitiful clenched hands, the miserable courage of these poor devils, the desperate charges and attacks made by these poor brave devils, who are so terrified that they dare not cry out loudly, but with battered chests and torn bellies and arms and legs only whimper softly for their mothers and cease as soon as one looks at them.

Their sharp, downy, dead faces have the awful expressionlessness of dead children.

It brings a lump into the throat to see how they go over, and run and fall. A man would like to spank them, they are so stupid, and to take them by the arm and lead them away from here where they have no business to be. They wear grey coats and trousers and boots, but for most of them the uniform is far too big, it hangs on their limbs, their shoulders are too narrow, their bodies too slight; no uniform was ever made to these childish measurements.

Between five and ten recruits fall to every old hand.

A surprise gas-attack carries off a lot of them. They have not yet learned what to do. We found one dug-out full of them, with blue heads and black lips. Some of them in a shell-hole took their masks off too soon; they did not know that the gas lies longest in the hollows; when they saw others on top without masks they pulled theirs off too and swallowed enough to scorch their lungs. Their condition is hopeless, they choke to death with hæmorrhages and suffocation.

In one part of the trench I suddenly run into Himmelstoss. We dive into the same dug-out. Breathless we are all lying one beside the other waiting for the charge.

When we run out again, although I am very excited, I suddenly think: "Where's Himmelstoss?" Quickly I jump back into the dug-out and find him with a small scratch lying in a corner pretending to be wounded. His face looks sullen. He is in a panic; he is new to it too. But it makes me mad that the young recruits should be out there and he here.

"Get out!" I spit.

He does not stir, his lips quiver, his moustache twitches.

"Out!" I repeat.

He draws up his legs, crouches back against the wall, and shows his teeth like a cur.

I seize him by the arm and try to pull him up. He barks.

That is too much for me. I grab him by the neck and shake him like a sack, his head jerks from side to side.

"You lump, will you get out – you hound, you skunk, sneak out of it, would you?" His eye becomes glassy, I knock his head against the wall – "You cow" – I kick him in the ribs – "You swine" – I push him toward the door and shove him out head first.

Another wave of our attack has just come up. A lieutenant is with them. He sees us and yells: "Forward, forward, join in, follow." And the word of command does what all my banging could not. Himmelstoss hears the order, looks round him as if awakened, and follows on.

I come after and watch him go over. Once more he is the smart Himmelstoss of the parade-ground, he has even outstripped the lieutenant and is far ahead.

Bombardment, barrage, curtain-fire, mines, gas, tanks, machine-guns, hand-grenades – words, words, but they hold the horror of the world.

Our faces are encrusted, our thoughts are devastated, we are weary to death; when the attack comes we shall have to strike many of the men with our fists to waken them and make them come with us – our eyes are burnt, our hands are torn, our knees bleed, our elbows are raw.

How long has it been? Weeks – months – years? Only days. We see time pass in the colourless faces of the dying, we cram food into us, we run, we throw, we shoot, we kill, we lie about, we are feeble and spent, and nothing supports us but the knowledge that there are still feebler, still more spent, still more helpless ones there who, with staring eyes, look upon us as gods that escape death many times.

In the few hours of rest we teach them. "There, see that waggle-top? That's a mortar coming. Keep down, it will go clean over. But if it comes this way, then run for it. You can run from a mortar."

We sharpen their ears to the malicious, hardly audible buzz of the smaller shells that are not so easily distinguished. They must pick them out from the general din by their insect-like hum – we explain to them that these are far more dangerous than the big ones that can be heard long beforehand.

We show them how to take cover from aircraft, how to simulate a dead man when one is overrun in an attack, how to time hand-grenades so that they explode half a second before hitting the ground; we teach them to fling themselves into holes as quick as lightning before the shells with instantaneous fuses; we show them how to clean up a trench with a handful of bombs; we explain the difference between the fuse-length of the enemy bombs and our own; we put them wise to the sound of gas shells; – show them all the tricks that can save them from death.

They listen, they are docile – but when it begins again, in their excitement they do everything wrong.

Haie Westhus drags off with a great wound in his back through which the lung pulses at every breath. I can only press his hand; "It's all up, Paul," he groans and bites his arm because of the pain.

We see men living with their skulls blown open; we see soldiers run with their two feet cut off, they stagger on their splintered stumps into the next shell-hole; a lance-corporal crawls a mile and half on his hands dragging his smashed knee after him; another goes to the dressing-station and over his clasped hands bulge his intestines; we see men without mouths, without jaws, without faces; we find one man who has held the artery of his arm in his teeth for two hours in order not to bleed to death. The sun goes down, night comes, the shells whine, life is at an end.

Still the little piece of convulsed earth in which we lie is held. We have yielded no more than a few hundred yards of it as a prize to the enemy. But on every yard there lies a dead man.

We have been relieved. The wheels roll beneath us, we stand dully, and when the call "Mind – wire" comes, we bend our knees. It was summer when we came up, the trees were still green, now it is autumn and the night is grey and wet. The lorries stop, we climb out – a confused heap, a remnant of many names. On either side stand people, dark, calling out the numbers of the regiments, the companies. And at each call a little group separates itself off, a small handful of dirty, pallid soldiers, a dreadfully small handful, and a dreadfully small remnant.

Now someone is calling the number of our company, it is, yes, the company commander, he has got one too, his arm is in a sling. We go over to him and I recognize Kat and Albert; we stand together, lean against each other, and look at one another.

And we hear the number of our company called again and again. He will call a long time, they do not hear him in the hospitals and shell-holes.

Once again: "Second Company, this way!"

And then more softly: "Nobody else Second Company?"

108

He is silent, and then huskily he says: "Is that all?" and gives the order: "Number!"

The morning is grey, it was still summer when we came up, and we were one hundred and fifty strong. Now we freeze, it is autumn, the leaves rustle, the voices flutter out wearily: "One – two – three – four – " and cease at thirty-two. And there is a long silence before the voice asks: "Anybody else?" – and waits and then says softly: "In squads –" and then breaks off and is only able to finish: "Second Company – " with difficulty: "Second Company – march easy!"

A line, a short line, trudges off into the morning.

Thirty-two men.

Chapter Seven

THEY HAVE TAKEN US farther back than usual to a field depot so that we can be re-organized. Our company needs more than a hundred reinforcements.

In the meantime, when we are off duty, we loaf around. After a couple of days Himmelstoss comes up to us. He has had the bounce knocked out of him since he has been in the trenches and wants to get on good terms with us. I am willing enough, because I saw how he brought Haie Westhus in when he was hit in the back. Besides he's decent enough to treat us at the canteen when we are out of funds. Only Tjaden is still reserved and suspicious.

But he is won over, too, when Himmelstoss tells us that he is taking the place of the sergeant-cook who has gone on leave. As a proof he produces on the spot two pounds of sugar for us and a half-pound of butter specially for Tjaden. He even sees to it that we are detailed the next two or three days to the cook-house for potato and turnip peeling. The grub he gives us there is real officers' fare.

Thus for the moment we have the two things a soldier needs for contentment: good food and rest. That's not much when one comes to think of it. A couple of years ago we would have despised ourselves terribly. But now we are quite happy. It is all a matter of habit – even the front-line.

Habit is the explanation of why we seem to forget things so quickly. Yesterday we were under fire, to-day we act the fool and go foraging through the countryside, to-morrow we go up to the trenches again. We forget nothing really. But so long as we have to stay here in the field, the front-line days, when they are past, sink down in us like a stone; they are too serious for us to be able to reflect on them at once. If we did that, we should have been destroyed long ago. I soon found out this much: – terror can be endured so long as a man simply ducks; – but it kills, if a man thinks about it.

Just as we turn into animals when we go up to the line, because that is the only thing which brings us through safely, so we turn into wags and loafers when we are out resting. We can do nothing else, it is a sheer necessity. We want to live at any price; so we cannot burden ourselves with feelings which, though they might be ornamental enough in peace time, would be out of place here. Kemmerich is dead, Haie Westhus is dying, they will have a job with Hans Kramer's body at the Judgment Day, piecing it together after a direct hit; Martens has no legs any more, Meyer is dead, Max is dead, Beyer is dead. Hämmerling is dead, there are a hundred and twenty wounded men lying somewhere or other; it is a damnable business, but what has it to do with us now – we live. If it were possible for us to save them, then it would be seen how much we cared – we would have a shot at it though we went under ourselves; for we can be damned quixotic when we like; fear we do not know much about – terror of death, yes; but that is a different matter, that is physical.

110

But our comrades are dead, we cannot help them, they have their rest – and who knows what is waiting for us? We will make ourselves comfortable and sleep, and eat as much as we can stuff into our bellies, and drink and smoke so that the hours are not wasted. Life is short.

The terror of the front sinks deep down when we turn our backs upon it; we make grim, coarse jests about it; that keeps us from going mad; as long as we take it that way we maintain our own resistance.

But we do not forget. It's all rot that they put in the war-news about the good humour of the troops, how they are arranging dances almost before they are out of the front-line. We don't act like that because we are in a good humour: we are in a good humour because otherwise we should go to pieces. If it were not so we could not hold out much longer; our humour becomes more bitter every month.

And this I know: all these things that now, while we are still in the war, sink down in us like a stone, after the war shall waken again, and then shall begin the disentanglement of life and death.

The days, the weeks, the years out here shall come back again, and our dead comrades shall then stand up again and march with us, our heads shall be clear, we shall have a purpose, and so we shall march, our dead comrades beside us, the years at the Front behind us: – against whom, against whom?

Some time ago there was an army theatre in these parts. Coloured posters of the performances are still sticking on a hoarding. With wide eyes Kropp and I stand in front of it. We can hardly credit that such things still exist. A girl in a light summer dress, with a red patent-leather belt about her hips! She is standing with one hand on a railing and with the other she holds a straw hat. She wears white stockings and white shoes, fine buckle shoes with high heels. Behind her smiles a blue lake with white-horses, at the side is a bright bay. She is a lovely girl with a delicate nose, red lips, and slender legs, wonderfully clean and well cared for, she certainly bathes twice a day and never has any dirt under her nails. At most perhaps a bit of sand from the beach.

Beside her stands a man in white trousers, a blue jacket, and sailor's cap; but he interests us much less.

The girl on the poster is a wonder to us. We have quite forgotten that there are such things, and even now we hardly believe our eyes. We have seen nothing like it for years, nothing like it for happiness, beauty, and joy. That is peace time, that is as it should be; we feel excited.

"Just look at those thin shoes though, she couldn't march many miles in those," I say, and then begin to feel silly, for it is absurd to stand in front of a picture like this and think of nothing but marching.

"How old would she be?" Kropp asks.

"About twenty-two at the most," I hazard.

"Then she would be older than us! She is not more than seventeen, let me tell you!"

It gives us goose-flesh.

"That would be good, Albert, what do you think?"

He nods. "I have white trousers at home too."

"White trousers," says I, "but a girl like that – "

We look askance at one another. There's not much to boast of here – two ragged, stained, and dirty uniforms. It is hopeless to compete.

So we proceed to tear the young man with the white trousers off the hoarding, taking care not to damage the girl. That is something towards it.

"We could go and get deloused, anyway," Kropp then suggests.

I am not very enthusiastic because it doesn't do one's clothes any good and a man is lousy again inside two hours. But when we have considered the picture once more, I declare myself willing. I even go farther.

"We might see if we could get a clean shirt as well – "

"Socks might be better," says Albert, not without reason.

"Yes, socks too perhaps. Let's go and explore a bit."

Then Leer and Tjaden stroll up; they look at the poster and immediately the conversation becomes smutty. Leer was the first of our class to have intercourse, and he gave stirring details of it. After his fashion he enjoys himself over the picture, and Tjaden supports him nobly.

It does not distress us exactly. Who isn't smutty is no soldier; it merely does not suit us at the moment, so we edge away and march off to the delousing station with the same feeling as if it were a swell gentlemen's outfitters.

The houses in which we are billeted lie near the canal. On the other side of the canal there are ponds flanked with poplars; – on the other side of the canal there are women too.

The houses on our side have been abandoned. On the other side though one occasionally sees inhabitants.

In the evening we go swimming. Three women come strolling along the bank. They walk slowly and don't look away, although we have no bathing suits.

Leer calls out to them. They laugh and stop to watch us. We fling remarks at them in broken French, anything that comes into our heads, hastily and all jumbled together, anything to detain them. They are not specially wonderful pieces, but then where are such to be had about here?

There is one slim little brunette. Her teeth gleam when she laughs. She has quick movements, her dress swings loosely about her legs. Although the water is cold we are very jovial and do our best to interest them so that they will stay. We try to make jokes and they answer with things we cannot understand; we laugh and beckon. Tjaden is more crafty. He runs into the house, gets a loaf of army bread and holds it up.

That produces a great effect. They nod and beckon us to come over. But we don't dare to do that. It is forbidden to cross to the opposite bank. There are sentries on all the bridges. It's impossible without a pass. So we indicate that they should come over to us; but they shake their heads and point to the bridge. They are not allowed to pass either. They turn away and walk slowly down the canal, keeping along the tow-path all the way. We accompany them swimming. After a few hundred yards they turn off and point to a house that stands a little distance away among the trees and shrubbery.

Leer asks if they live there.

They laugh – sure, that's their house.

114

We call out to them that we would like to come, sometime when the guards cannot see us. At night. To-night.

They raise their hands, put them together, rest their faces on them and shut their eyes. They understand. The slim brunette does a two-step. The blonde girl twitters: "Bread – good – "

Eagerly we assure them that we will bring some with us. And other tasty bits too, we roll our eyes and try to explain with our hands. Leer nearly drowns trying to demonstrate a sausage. If it were necessary we would promise them a whole quartermaster's store. They go off and frequently turn and look back. We climb out on the bank on our side of the canal and watch to see whether they go into the house for they might easily have been lying. Then we swim back.

No one can cross the bridge without leave, so we will simply have to swim over at night. We are full of excitement. We cannot last out without a drink, so we go to the canteen where there is beer and a kind of punch.

We drink punch and tell one another lying tales of our experiences. Each man gladly believes the other man's story, only waiting impatiently till he can cap it with a taller one. Our hands are fidgety, we smoke countless cigarettes, until Kropp says: "We might as well take them a couple of cigarettes too." So we put some inside our caps to keep them.

The sky turns apple-green. There are four of us, but only three can go; we must shake off Tjaden, so ply him with rum and punch until he rocks. As it turns dark we go to our billets, Tjaden in the centre. We are all glowing and full of a lust for adventure. The little brunette is mine, we settled that by cutting for her.

Tjaden drops on his sack of straw and snores. Once he wakes up and grins so craftily that we are alarmed and begin to think he is cheating, and that we have given him the punch to no purpose. Then he drops back again and sleeps on.

We each get hold of a whole army loaf and wrap it up in newspaper. The cigarettes we put in too, as well as three good rations of liver-sausage that were issued to us this evening. That makes a decent present.

We stow the things carefully in our boots; we have to take them to protect our feet against treading on wire and broken glass on the other bank. As we must swim for it we can take no other clothes. But it is not far and quite dark.

We make off with our boots in our hands. Swiftly we slip into the water, lie on our backs and swim, holding the boots with their contents up over our heads.

We climb out carefully on the opposite bank, take out the packages and put on our boots. We put the things under our arms. And so, all wet and naked, clothed only in our boots, we break into a trot. We find the house at once. It lies among the trees. Leer trips over a root and skins his elbows.

"No matter," he says gaily.

The windows are shuttered. We slip round the house and try to peer through the cracks. Then we grow impatient. Suddenly Kropp hesitates:

"What if there's a Major in with them?"

"Then we just clear off," grins Leer, "he can try to read our regimental numbers here," and smacks his behind.

The door of the courtyard stands open. Our boots make a great

116

clatter. The house door opens, a chink of light shines through and a woman cries out in a scared voice.

"Ssh, ssh! *camerade – bon ami –*" we say, and show our packages protestingly.

The other two are now on the scene, the door opens wide and the light floods over us. They recognize us and all three burst into laughter at our appearance. They rock and sway in the doorway, they laugh so much. How supple their movements are!

"*Un moment –*" They disappear and throw us bits of clothing which we gladly wrap round ourselves. Then we venture in. A small lamp burns in the room, which is warm and smells a little of perfume. We unwrap our parcels and hand them over to the women. Their eyes shine, it is obvious that they are hungry.

Then we all become rather embarrassed. Leer makes the gestures of eating, and then they come to life again and bring out plates and knives and fall to on the food, and they hold up every slice of liver-sausage and admire it before they eat it, and we sit proudly by.

They overwhelm us with their chatter; – we understand very little of it, but we listen and the words sound friendly. No doubt we all look very young. The little brunette strokes my hair and says what all the French women say: "*La guerre – grand malheur – pauvres garçons –*"

I hold her arm tightly and press my lips into the palm of her hand. Her fingers close round my face. Close above me are her bewildering eyes, the soft brown of her skin and her red lips. Her mouth speaks words I do not understand. Nor do I fully understand her eyes; they seem to say more than we anticipated when we came here.

There are other rooms adjoining. In passing I see Leer, he has made a great hit with the blonde. And he knows it, too. But I – I am lost in remoteness, in weakness, and in a passion to which I yield myself trustingly. My desires are strangely compounded of yearning and misery. I feel giddy, there is nothing here that a man can hold on to. We have left our boots at the door, they have given us slippers instead, and now nothing remains to recall for me the assurance and self-confidence of the soldier; no rifle, no belt, no tunic, no cap. I let myself drop into the unknown, come what may – yet, in spite of all, I feel somewhat afraid.

The little brunette contracts her brows when she is thinking; but when she talks they are still. And often the sound does not quite become a word but suffocates or floats away over me half-finished; an arch, a pathway, a comet. What have I known of it – what do I know of it? – The words of this foreign tongue, that I hardly understand, they caress me to a quietness, in which the room grows dim, and dissolves in the half light, and only the face above me lives and is clear.

How various is a face; but an hour ago it was strange and now it is touched with a tenderness that comes, not from it, but out of the night, the world and the blood, all these things seem to shine in it together. The objects in the room are touched by it and transformed, they be-

118

come isolated, and I feel almost awed at the sight of my clear skin when the light of the lamp falls upon it and the cool, brown hand passes over it.

How different all this is from the conditions in the soldiers' brothels, to which we are allowed to go, and where we have to wait in long queues. I wish I never thought of them; but desire turns my mind to them involuntarily and I am afraid, for it might be impossible ever to be free of them again.

But then I feel the lips of the little brunette and press myself against them, my eyes close and I let it all fall from me, war and terror and grossness, in order to awaken young and happy; I think of the picture of the girl on the poster and, for a moment, believe that my life depends on winning her. And if I press ever deeper into the arms that embrace me, perhaps a miracle may happen. . . .

So, after a time we find ourselves reassembled again. Leer is in high spirits. We pull on our boots and take our leave warmly. The night air cools our hot bodies. The rustling poplars loom large in the darkness. The moon floats in the heavens and in the waters of the canal. We do not run, we walk beside one another with long strides.

"That was worth a ration-loaf," says Leer.

I cannot trust myself to speak, I am not in the least happy.

Then we hear footsteps and dodge behind a shrub.

The steps come nearer, close by us. We see a naked soldier, in boots, just like ourselves; he has a package under his arm, and gallops onward. It is Tjaden in full course. He has disappeared already.

We laugh. In the morning he will curse us. Unobserved, we arrive again at our sacks of straw.

I am called to the Orderly Room. The company commander gives me a leave-pass and a travel-pass and wishes me a good journey. I look to see how much leave I have got. Seventeen days – fourteen days leave and three days for travelling. It is not enough and I ask whether I cannot have five days for travelling. Bertinck points to my pass. There I see that I am not to return to the front immediately. After my leave I have to report for a course of training to a camp on the moors.

The others congratulate me. Kat gives me good advice, and tells me I ought to try to get a base-job. "If you are smart, you'll hang on to it."

I would rather not have gone for another eight days; we are to stay here that much longer and it is good here.

Naturally I have to stand the others drinks at the canteen. We are all a little bit drunk. I become gloomy: I will be away for six weeks – That is lucky of course, but what may happen before I get back? Shall I meet all these fellows again? Already Haie has gone – who will the next be?

As we drink, I look at each of them in turn. Albert sits beside me and smokes, he is silent, we have always been together – opposite squats Kat, with his drooping shoulders, his broad thumb, and calm voice – Müller with the protruding teeth and the booming laugh – Tjaden with his mousy eyes – Leer who has grown a full beard and looks at least forty.

Over us hangs a dense cloud of smoke. Where would a soldier be without tobacco? The canteen is his refuge, and beer is far more than a drink, it is a token that a man can move his limbs and stretch in safety. We do it ceremonially, we stretch our legs out in front of us and spit deliberately, that is the only way. How it all rises up before a man when he is going away the next morning!

At night we go again to the other side of the canal. I am almost afraid to tell the little brunette that I am going away, and when I return we will certainly be far away from here; we will never see one another again. But she merely nods and takes no special notice. At first I am at a loss to understand, then it suddenly dawns on me. Yes, Leer is right: if I were going up to the front, then she would have again called me *"pauvre garçon"*; but merely going on leave – she does not want to hear about that, that is not nearly so interesting. May she go to the devil with her chattering talk. A man dreams of a miracle and wakes up to loaves of bread.

Next morning, after I have been deloused, I go to the rail head. Albert and Kat come with me. At the halt we learn that it will be a couple of hours yet before the train leaves. The other two have to go back to duty. We take leave of one another.

"Good luck, Kat; good luck, Albert."

They go off and wave once or twice. Their figures dwindle. I know their every step and movement; I would recognize them at any distance. Then they disappear. I sit down on my pack and wait.

Suddenly I become filled with a consuming impatience to be gone.

I lie down on many a station platform; I stand before many a soup-kitchen; I squat on many a bench; – then at last the landscape becomes gloomy, mysterious, and familiar. It glides past the western windows with its villages, their thatched roofs like caps, pulled over the white-washed, half-timbered houses, its corn-fields, gleaming like mother-of-pearl in the slanting light, its orchards, its barns and old lime trees.

The names of the stations begin to take on meaning and my heart trembles. The train stamps and stamps onward, I stand at the window and hold on to the frame. These names mark the boundaries of my youth.

Smooth meadows, fields, farmyards; a solitary team moves against the sky-line along the road that runs parallel to the horizon – a bar-

121

rier, before which peasants stand waiting, girls waving, children playing on the embankment, roads, leading into the country, smooth roads without artillery.

It is evening, and if the train did not rattle I should cry out. The plain unfolds itself.

In the distance, the soft, blue silhouette of the mountain ranges begins to appear. I recognize the characteristic outline of the Dolbenberg, a jagged comb, springing up precipitously from the limit of the forests. Behind it should lie the town.

But now the sun streams through the world, dissolving everything in its golden-red light, the train swings round one curve and then another; – far away, in a long line one behind the other, stand the poplars, unsubstantial, swaying and dark, fashioned out of shadow, light, and desire.

The field swings round as the train encircles it, and the intervals between the trees diminish; the trees become a block and for a moment I see one only – then they reappear from behind the foremost tree and stand out a long line against the sky until they are hidden by the first houses.

A street-crossing. I stand at the window, I cannot drag myself away. The others put their baggage ready for getting out. I repeat to myself the name of the Street that we cross over – Bremerstrasse – Bremerstrasse –

Below there are cyclists, lorries, men; it is a grey street and a grey subway; – it embraces me as though it were my mother.

Then the train stops, and there is the station with noise and cries and sentries. I pick up my pack and fasten the straps, I take my rifle in my hand and stumble down the steps.

On the platform I look round; I know no one among the people hurrying to and fro. A Red Cross sister offers me something to drink. I turn away, she smiles at me too foolishly, so obsessed with her own importance: "Just look, I am giving a soldier coffee!" – She calls me "Comrade," but I will have none of it.

Outside in front of the station the stream roars alongside the street, it rushes foaming from the sluices of the mill bridge. There stands the old, square watch-tower, in front of it the great mottled lime tree and behind it the evening.

Here we have often sat – how long ago it is – we have passed over this bridge and breathed the cool, acid smell of the stagnant water; we have leaned over the still water on this side of the lock, where the green creepers and weeds hang from the piles of the bridge; – and on hot days we rejoiced in the spouting foam on the other side of the lock and told tales about our school-teachers.

I pass over the bridge, I look right and left; the water is as full of weeds as ever, and it still shoots over in gleaming arches; in the tower-building laundresses still stand with bare arms as they used to over the clean linen, and the heat from the ironing pours out through the open windows. Dogs trot along the narrow street, before the doors of the houses people stand and follow me with their gaze as I pass by, dirty and heavy laden.

In this confectioner's we used to eat ices, and there we learned to smoke cigarettes. Walking down the street I know every shop, the colonial warehouses, the chemist's, the tobacconist's. Then at last I stand before the brown door with its worn latch and my hand grows heavy. I open the door and a wonderful freshness comes out to meet me, my eyes are dim.

The stairs creak under my boots. Upstairs a door rattles, someone is looking over the railing. It is the kitchen door that was opened, they are cooking potato-cakes, the house reeks of it, and to-day of course is Saturday; that will be my sister leaning over. For a moment I am shy and lower my head, then I take off my helmet and look up. Yes, it is my eldest sister.

"Paul," she cries, "Paul – "

I nod, my pack bumps against the banisters; my rifle is so heavy.

She pulls a door open and calls: "Mother, Mother, Paul is here."

I can go no further – Mother, Mother, Paul is here.

I lean against the wall and grip my helmet and rifle. I hold them as tight as I can, but I cannot take another step, the staircase fades before

124

my eyes, I support myself with the butt of my rifle against my feet and clench my teeth fiercely, but I cannot speak a word, my sister's call has made me powerless, I can do nothing, I struggle to make myself laugh, to speak, but no word comes, and so I stand on the steps, miserable, helpless, paralyzed, and against my will the tears run down my cheeks.

My sister comes back and says: "Why, what is the matter?"

Then I pull myself together and stagger on to the landing. I lean my rifle in a corner, I set my pack against the wall, place my helmet on it, and fling down my equipment and baggage. Then I say fiercely: "Bring me a handkerchief."

She gives me one from the cupboard and I dry my face. Above me on the wall hangs the glass case with the coloured butterflies that once I collected.

Now I hear my mother's voice. It comes from the bedroom.

"Is she in bed?" I ask my sister.

"She is ill – " she replies.

I go in to her, give her my hand and say as calmly as I can: "Here I am, Mother."

She lies still in the dim light. Then she asks anxiously:

"Are you wounded?" and I feel her searching glance.

"No, I have got leave."

My mother is very pale. I am afraid to make a light.

"Here I lie now," says she, "and cry instead of being glad."

"Are you sick, Mother?" I ask.

"I am going to get up a little to-day," she says and turns to my sister, who is continually running to the kitchen to watch that the food does not burn: "And put out the jar of preserved whortleberries – you like that, don't you?" she asks me.

"Yes, Mother, I haven't had any for a long time."

"We might almost have known you were coming," laughs my sister,

125

"there is just your favourite dish, potato-cakes, and even whortle-berries to go with them too."

"And it is Saturday," I add.

"Sit here beside me," says my mother.

She looks at me. Her hands are white and sickly and frail compared with mine. We say very little, and I am thankful that she asks nothing. What ought I to say? Everything I could have wished for has happened. I have come out of it safely and sit here beside her. And in the kitchen stands my sister making the evening bread and singing.

"Dear boy," says my mother softly.

We were never very demonstrative in our family; poor folk who toil and are full of cares are not so. It is not their way to protest what they already know. When my mother says to me "dear boy," it means much more than when another uses it. I know well enough that the jar of whortleberries is the only one they have had for months, and that she has kept it for me; and the somewhat stale cakes that she gives me too. She has taken a favourable opportunity of getting a few and has put them all by for me.

I sit by her bed, and through the window the chestnut trees in the beer-garden opposite glow in brown and gold. I breathe deeply and say over to myself: – "You are at home, you are at home." But a sense of strangeness will not leave me, I can find nothing of myself in all these things. There is my mother, there is my sister, there my case of butterflies, and there the mahogany piano – but I am not myself there. There is a distance, a veil between us.

I go and fetch my pack to the bedside and turn out the things I have brought – a whole Edam cheese, that Kat provided me with, two loaves of army bread, three-quarters of a pound of butter, two tins of liver-sausage, a pound of dripping and a little bag of rice.

"I suppose you can make some use of that – "

They nod.

126

"Is it pretty bad for food here?" I enquire.

"Yes, there's not much. Do you get enough out there?"

I smile and point to the things I have brought. "Not always quite so much as that, of course, but we fare reasonably well."

Erna goes out to bring in the food. Suddenly my mother seizes hold of my hand and asks falteringly: "Was it very bad out there, Paul?"

Mother, what should I answer to that! You would not understand, and never realize it. And you never should realize it. Was it bad, you ask. – You, Mother, – I shake my head and say: "No, Mother, not so very. There are always a lot of us together so it isn't so bad."

"Yes, but Heinrich Bredemeyer was here just lately and he said it was terrible out there now, with the gas and all the rest of it."

It is my mother who says that. She says: "With the gas and all the rest of it." She does not know what she is saying, she is merely anxious for me. Should I tell her how we once found three enemy trenches with their garrison all stiff as though stricken with apoplexy? Against the parapet, in the dug-outs, just where they were, the men stood and lay about, with blue faces, dead.

"No, Mother, that's only talk," I answer, "there's not very much in what Bredemeyer says. You see for instance, I'm well and fit – "

Before my mother's tremulous anxiety I recover my composure. Now I can walk about and talk and answer questions without fear of having suddenly to lean against the wall because the world turns soft as rubber and my veins become brimstone.

My mother wants to get up. So I go for a while to my sister in the kitchen. "What is the matter with her?" I ask.

She shrugs her shoulders: "She has been in bed two months now, but we did not want to write and tell you. Several doctors have been to see her. One of them said it is probably cancer again."

I go to the District Commandant to report myself. Slowly I wander

127

through the streets. Occasionally someone speaks to me. I do not delay long for I have little inclination to talk.

On my way back from the barracks a loud voice calls out to me. Still lost in thought I turn round and find myself confronted by a Major. "Can't you salute?" he blusters.

"Sorry, Major," I say in embarrassment, "I didn't notice you."

"Don't you know how to speak properly?" he roars.

I would like to hit him in the face, but control myself, for my leave depends on it. I click my heels and say: "I did not see you, Herr Major."

"Then keep your eyes open," he snorts. "What is your name?" I give it.

His fat red face is furious. "What regiment?"

I give him full particulars. Even yet he has not had enough. "Where are they?"

But I had had more than enough and say: "Between Langemark and Bixschoote."

"Eh?" he asks, a bit stupefied.

I explain to him that I arrived on leave only an hour or two since, thinking that he would then trot along. But not at all. He gets even

128

more furious: "You think you can bring your front-line manners here, what? Well, we don't stand that sort of thing. Thank God, we have discipline here!

"Twenty paces backwards, double march!" he commands.

I am mad with rage. But I cannot say anything to him; he could put me under arrest if he liked. So I double back, and then march up to him. Six paces from him I spring to a stiff salute and maintain it until I am six paces beyond him.

He calls me back again and affably gives me to understand that for once he is pleased to put mercy before justice. I pretend to be duly grateful. "Now, dismiss!" he says. I turn about smartly and march off.

That ruins the evening for me. I go back home and throw my uniform into a corner; I ought to have done that before. Then I take out my civilian clothes from the wardrobe and put them on.

I feel awkward. The suit is rather tight and short, I have grown in the army. Collar and tie give me some trouble. In the end my sister ties the bow for me. But how light the suit is, it feels as though I had nothing on but a shirt and underpants.

I look at myself in the glass. It is a strange sight. A sunburnt, over-grown candidate for confirmation gazes at me in astonishment.

My mother is pleased to see me wearing civilian clothes; it makes me less strange to her. But my father would rather I kept my uniform on so that he could take me to visit his acquaintances.

But I refuse.

It is pleasant to sit quietly somewhere, in the beer-garden for example, under the chestnuts by the skittle-alley. The leaves fall down on the table and on the ground, only a few, the first. A glass of beer stands in front of me, I've learned to drink in the army. The glass is half empty, but there are still a few good swigs ahead of me, and besides I can always order a second and a third if I wish to. There are no

129

bugles and no bombardments, the children of the house play in the skittle-alley, and the dog rests his head against my knee. The sky is blue, between the leaves of the chestnuts rises the green spire of St. Margaret's Church.

This is good, I like it. But I cannot get on with the people. My mother is the only one who asks no questions. Not so my father. He wants me to tell him about the front; he is curious in a way that I find stupid and distressing; I no longer have any real contact with him. There is nothing he likes more than just hearing about it. I realize he does not know that a man cannot talk of such things; I would do it willingly, but it is too dangerous for me to put these things into words. I am afraid they might then become gigantic and I be no longer able to master them. What would become of us if everything that happens out there were quite clear to us?

So I confine myself to telling him a few amusing things. But he wants to know whether I have ever had a hand-to-hand fight. I say "No," and get up and go out.

But that does not mend matters. After I have been startled a couple of times in the street by the screaming of the tramcars, which resembles the shriek of a shell coming straight for one, somebody taps me on the shoulder. It is my German-master, and he fastens on me with the usual question: "Well, how are things out there? Terrible, terrible, eh? Yes, it is dreadful, but we must carry on. And after all, you do at least get decent food out there, so I hear. You look well, Paul, and fit. Naturally it's worse here. Naturally. The best for our soldiers every time, that goes without saying."

He drags me along to a table with a lot of others. They welcome me, a head-master shakes hands with me and says: "So you come from the front? What is the spirit like out there? Excellent, eh? Excellent?"

I explain that no one would be sorry to be back home.

He laughs uproariously. "I can well believe it! But first you have to give the Froggies a good hiding. Do you smoke? Here, try one. Waiter, bring a beer as well for our young warrior."

Unfortunately I have accepted the cigar, so I have to remain. And they are all so dripping with good will that it is impossible to object. All the same I feel annoyed and smoke like a chimney as hard as I can. In order to make at least some show of appreciation I toss off the beer in one gulp. Immediately a second is ordered; people know how much they are indebted to the soldiers. They argue about what we ought to annex. The head-master with the steel watch-chain wants to have at least the whole of Belgium, the coal-areas of France, and a slice of Russia. He produces reasons why we must have them and is quite inflexible until at last the others give in to him. Then he begins to expound just whereabouts in France the break-through must come, and turns to me: "Now, shove ahead a bit out there with your ever-lasting trench warfare – Smash through the Johnnies and then there will be peace."

I reply that in our opinion a break-through may not be possible. The enemy may have too many reserves. Besides, the war may be rather different from what people think.

He dismisses the idea loftily and informs me I know nothing about it. "The details, yes," says he, "but this relates to the whole. And of that you are not able to judge. You see only your little sector and so cannot have any general survey. You do your duty, you risk your lives, that deserves the highest honour – every man of you ought to have the Iron Cross – but first of all the enemy line must be broken through in Flanders and then rolled up from the top."

He blows his nose and wipes his beard. "Completely rolled up they must be, from the top to the bottom. And then to Paris."

I would like to know just how he pictures it to himself, and pour the third glass of beer into me. Immediately he orders another.

But I break away. He stuffs a few more cigars into my pocket and sends me off with a friendly slap. "All of the best! I hope we will soon hear something worth while from you."

I imagined leave would be different from this. Indeed, it was different a year ago. It is I of course that have changed in the interval. There lies a gulf between that time and to-day. At that time I still knew nothing about the war, we had been only in quiet sectors. But now I see that I have been crushed without knowing it. I find I do not belong here any more, it is a foreign world. Some of these people ask questions, some ask no questions, but one can see that they are quite confident they know all about it; they often say so with their air of comprehension, so there is no point in discussing it. They make up a picture of it for themselves.

I prefer to be alone, so that no one troubles me. For they all come back to the same thing, how badly it goes and how well it goes; one thinks it is this way, another that; and yet they are always absorbed in the things that go to make up their own existence. Formerly I lived in just the same way myself, but now I feel no contact here any longer.

They talk to me too much. They have worries, aims, desires, that I cannot comprehend. I often sit with one of them in the little beer-garden and try to explain to him that this is really the only thing: just to sit quietly, like this. They understand of course, they agree, they may even feel it so too, but only with words, only with words, yes,

132

that is it – they feel it, but always with only half of themselves, the rest of their being is taken up with other things, they are so divided in themselves that none feels it with his whole essence; I cannot even say myself exactly what I mean.

When I see them here, in their rooms, in their offices, about their occupations, I feel an irresistible attraction in it, I would like to be here too and forget the war; but also it repels me, it is so narrow, how can that fill a man's life, he ought to smash it to bits; how can they do it, while out at the front the splinters are whining over the shell-holes and the star-shells go up, the wounded are carried back on waterproof sheets and comrades crouch in the trenches. – They are different men here, men I cannot properly understand, whom I envy and despise. I must think of Kat and Albert and Müller and Tjaden, what will they be doing? No doubt they are sitting in the canteen, or perhaps swimming – soon they will have to go up to the front-line again.

In my room behind the table stands a brown leather sofa. I sit down on it.

On the walls are pasted countless pictures that I once used to cut out of the newspapers. In between are drawings and postcards that have come my way. In the corner is a small iron stove. Against the wall opposite stand the book-shelves with my books.

I used to live in this room before I was a soldier. The books I bought gradually with money I earned by coaching. Many of them are second-hand, all the classics for example, one volume in blue cloth boards cost one mark twenty pfennig. I bought them complete because I was thoroughgoing, I did not trust the editors of selections, even though they may have chosen all the best. So I purchased only "collected works." I read most of them with laudable zeal, but few of them really appealed to me. I preferred the other books, the moderns, which were of course much dearer. A few I came by not quite honestly, I borrowed and did not return them because I did not want to part with them.

One shelf is filled with school books. They are not so well cared for, they are badly thumbed, and pages have been torn out for certain purposes. Then below are periodicals, papers, and letters all jammed in together with drawings and rough sketches.

I want to think myself back into that time. It is still in the room, I feel it at once, the walls have preserved it. My hands rest on the arms of the sofa; now I make myself at home and draw up my legs so that I sit comfortably in the corner, in the arms of the sofa. The little window is open, through it I see the familiar picture of the street with the rising spire of the church at the end. There are a couple of flowers on the table. Pen-holders, a shell as a paper-weight, the ink-well – here nothing is changed.

It will be like this too, if I am lucky, when the war is over and I come back here for good. I will sit here just like this and look at my room and wait.

I feel excited; but I do not want to be, for that is not right. I want that quiet rapture again. I want to feel the same powerful, nameless urge that I used to feel when I turned to my books. The breath of desire that then arose from the coloured backs of the books shall fill me again, melt the heavy, dead lump of lead that lies somewhere in me and waken again the impatience for the future, the quick joy in the world of thought, it shall bring back again the lost eagerness of my youth. I sit and wait.

It occurs to me that I must go and see Kemmerich's mother; – I might visit Mittelstaedt too, he should be at the barracks. I look out of the window; – beyond the sober picture of the street appears a range of hills, distant and light; it changes to a clear day in autumn, and I sit by the fire with Kat and Albert and eat potatoes baked in their skins.

But I do not want to think of that, I sweep it away. The room shall speak, it must catch me up and hold me, I want to feel that I belong here, I want to hearken and know when I go back to the front that the

134

war will sink down, be drowned utterly in the great home-coming tide, know that it will then be past for ever, and not gnaw us continually, that it will have none but an outward power over us.

The backs of the books stand in rows. I know them all still, I remember arranging them in order. I implore them with my eyes: Speak to me – take me up – take me, Life of my Youth – you who are carefree, beautiful – receive me again –

I wait, I wait.

Images float through my mind, but they do not grip me, they are mere shadows and memories.

Nothing – nothing –

My disquietude grows.

A terrible feeling of foreignness suddenly rises up in me. I cannot find my way back, I am shut out though I entreat earnestly and put forth all my strength.

Nothing stirs; listless and wretched, like a condemned man, I sit there and the past withdraws itself. And at the same time I fear to importune it too much, because I do not know what might happen then. I am a soldier, I must cling to that.

Wearily I stand up and look out of the window. Then I take one of the books, intending to read, and turn over the leaves. But I put it away and take out another. There are passages in it that have been marked. I look, turn over the pages, take up fresh books. Already they are piled up beside me. Speedily more join the heap, papers, magazines, letters.

I stand there dumb. As before a judge.

Dejected.

Words, Words, Words – they do not reach me.

Slowly I place the books back in the shelves.

Nevermore.

Quietly, I go out of the room.

Still I do not give up hope. I do not, indeed, go to my room any more, but comfort myself with the thought that a few days are not enough to judge by. Afterwards – later on – there is plenty of time for that.

So I go over to see Mittelstaedt in the barracks, and we sit in his room; there is an atmosphere about it that I do not like but with which I am quite familiar.

Mittelstaedt has some news ready for me that electrifies me on the spot. He tells me Kantorek has been called up as a territorial.

"Just think of it," says he, and takes out a couple of good cigars, "I come back here from the hospital and bump right into him. He stretches out his paw to me and bleats: 'Hullo Mittelstaedt, how are you?' – I look at him and say: 'Territorial Kantorek, business is business and schnapps is schnapps, you ought to know that well enough yourself. Stand to attention when you speak to a superior officer.' You should have seen his face! A cross between a dud and a pickled cucumber. He tried once again to chum up. So I snubbed him a bit harder. Then he brought up his biggest guns and asked confidentially: 'Would you like me to use my influence so that you can take an emergency-exam?' He was trying to remind me of those things, you know. Then I got mad and I reminded him of something instead. 'Territorial Kantorek, two years ago you preached us into enlisting; and among us there was one, Joseph Behm, who didn't want to enlist. He was killed three months before he would have been called up in the ordinary way. If it had not been for you he would have lived just that much longer. And now: Dismiss. You will hear from me later.' It was easy to get put in charge of his company. First thing I did was to take him to the stores and fit him out with a suitable equipment. You will see in a minute."

We go out to the parade-ground. The company has fallen in. Mittelstaedt stands them at ease and inspects.

Then I see Kantorek and am scarcely able to stifle my laughter. He is wearing a faded blue tunic. On the back and in the sleeves there

136

are big dark patches. The overcoat must have belonged to a giant. The black, worn breeches are just as much too short; they reach barely halfway down his calf. The boots, tough old clod-hoppers, with turned-up toes and laces at the side, are much too big for him. But as a compensation the cap is too small, a terribly dirty, mean little pill-box. The whole rig-out is just pitiful.

Mittelstaedt stops in front of him: "Territorial Kantorek, do you call those buttons polished? You seem as if you can never learn. Inadequate, Kantorek, quite inadequate – "

It makes me bubble with glee. In school Kantorek used to chasten Mittelstaedt with exactly the same expression – "Inadequate, Mittelstaedt, quite inadequate."

Mittelstaedt continues to upbraid him: "Look at Boettcher now, there's a model for you to learn from."

I can hardly believe my eyes. Boettcher is there too, Boettcher, our school porter. And he is a model! Kantorek shoots a glance at me as if he would like to eat me. But I grin at him innocently, as though I do not recognize him any more.

Nothing could look more ludicrous than his forage-cap and his uniform. And this is the object before whom we used to stand in anguish, as he sat up there enthroned at his desk, spearing at us with his pencil for our mistakes in those irregular French verbs with which afterwards we made so little headway in France. That is barely two years ago – and now here stands Territorial Kantorek, the spell quite broken, with bent knees, arms like pothooks, unpolished buttons and that ludicrous rig-out – an impossible soldier. I cannot reconcile this with the menacing figure at the schoolmaster's desk. I wonder what I, the old soldier, would do if this skin full of woe ever dared to say to me again: "Bäumer, give the imperfect of 'aller.' "

Then Mittelstaedt makes them practise skirmishing, and as a favour appoints Kantorek squad leader.

Now in skirmishing the squad leader has always to keep twenty paces in front of his squad; if the order comes, "On the march, about turn," the line of skirmishers simply turns about, but the squad leader, who now finds himself suddenly twenty paces in rear of the line, has to rush up at the double and take his position again twenty paces in front of the squad. That makes altogether forty paces double-march. But no sooner has he arrived than the order, "On the march, about turn," comes again and he once more has to race at top speed another forty paces to the other side. In this way the squad has made merely the turn-about and a couple of paces while the squad leader dashes backwards and forwards. That is one of Himmelstoss's well-worn recipes.

Kantorek can hardly expect anything else from Mittelstaedt, for he once messed up the latter's chance of promotion, and Mittelstaedt would be a big fool not to make the best of such a good opportunity as this, before he goes back to the front again. A man might well die easier after the army has given him just one such stroke of luck.

In the meantime Kantorek is dashing up and down like a wild-boar. After a while Mittelstaedt stops the skirmish and begins the very important exercise of creeping.

On hands and knees, carrying his gun in regulation fashion, Kantorek shoves his absurd figure over the sand immediately in front of us. He is breathing hard, and his panting is music.

Mittelstaedt encourages Kantorek the Territorial with quotations from Kantorek the Schoolmaster. "Territorial Kantorek, we have the good fortune to live in a great age, we must all humble ourselves and for once put aside bitterness."

Kantorek sweats and spits out a dirty piece of wood that has lodged in his teeth.

Mittelstaedt stoops down and says reproachfully: "And in the trifles never lose sight of the great adventure, Territorial Kantorek!"

It amazes me that Kantorek does not explode with a bang, especially when, during physical exercises, Mittelstaedt copies him to perfection, seizing him by the seat of his trousers as he is climbing along the horizontal bar, so that he can just raise his chin above the beam, and then starts to give him good advice. That is exactly what Kantorek used to do to him at school.

The extra fatigues are next detailed off. "Kantorek and Boettcher, bread fatigue! Take the handcart with you."

In a couple of minutes the two set off together pushing the barrow. Kantorek in a fury walks with his head down. But the porter is delighted to have scored light duty.

The bakehouse is away at the other end of the town, and the two must go there and back through the whole length of it.

"They've done that a couple of times already," grins Mittelstaedt. "There are still a few people waiting to see them."

"Excellent," I say, "but hasn't he reported you yet?"

"He did try. Our C.O. laughed like the deuce when he heard the story. He hasn't any time for schoolmasters. Besides, I'm sweet with his daughter."

"He'll mess up the examination for you."

"I don't care," says Mittelstaedt calmly. "Besides, his complaint came to nothing because I could show that he had had hardly anything but light duty."

"Couldn't you polish him up a bit?" I ask.

"He's too stupid, I couldn't be bothered," answers Mittelstaedt contemptuously.

What is leave? – A pause that only makes everything after it so much worse. Already the sense of parting begins to intrude itself. My mother watches me silently; – I know she counts the days; – every morning she is sad. It is one day less. She has put away my pack, she does not want to be reminded by it.

The hours pass quickly if a man broods. I pull myself together, and go with my sister to the butcher's to get a pound of bones. That is a great luxury and people line up early in the morning and stand waiting. Many of them faint.

We have no luck. After waiting by turns for three hours the queue disperses. The bones have not lasted out.

It is a good thing I get my rations. I bring them to my mother and in that way we all get something decent to eat.

The days grow ever more strained and my mother's eyes more sorrowful. Four days left now. I must go and see Kemmerich's mother.

I cannot write that down. This quaking, sobbing woman who shakes me and cries out at me: "Why are you living then, when he is dead?" – who drowns me in tears and calls out: "What are you there for at all, child, when you – " – who drops into a chair and wails: "Did you see him? Did you see him then? How did he die?"

140

I tell her he was shot through the heart and died instantaneously. She looks at me, she doubts me: "You lie. I know better. I have felt how terribly he died. I have heard his voice at night, I have felt his anguish – tell the truth, I want to know it, I must know it."

"No," I say, "I was beside him. He died at once."

She pleads with me gently: "Tell me. You must tell me. I know you want to comfort me, but don't you see, you torment me far more than if you told me the truth? I cannot bear the uncertainty. Tell me how it was and even though it will be terrible, it will be far better than what I have to think if you don't."

I will never tell her, she can make mince-meat out of me first. I console her, but she strikes me as rather stupid all the same. Why doesn't she stop worrying? Kemmerich will stay dead whether she knows about it or not. When a man has seen so many dead he cannot understand any longer why there should be so much anguish over a single individual. So I say rather impatiently: "He died immediately. He felt absolutely nothing at all. His face was quite calm."

She is silent. Then she says slowly: "Will you swear it?"

"Yes."

"By everything that is sacred to you?"

Good God, what is there that is sacred to me? – such things change pretty quickly with us. "Yes, he died at once."

"Are you willing never to come back yourself, if it isn't true?"

"May I never come back if he wasn't killed instantaneously."

I would swear to anything. But she seems to believe me. She moans and weeps steadily. I have to tell how it happened so I invent a story and I almost believe it myself.

As I leave she kisses me and gives me a picture of him. In his recruit's uniform he leans on a round rustic table with legs made of birch branches. Behind him a wood is painted on a curtain, and on the table stands a mug of beer.

141

It is the last evening at home. Everyone is silent. I go to bed early, I seize the pillow, press it against myself and bury my head in it. Who knows if I will ever lie in a feather bed again?

Late in the night my mother comes into my room. She thinks I am asleep, and I pretend to be so. To talk, to stay awake with one another, it is too hard.

She sits long into the night although she is in pain and often writhes. At last I can bear it no longer, and pretend I have just waked up.

"Go and sleep, Mother, you will catch cold here."

"I can sleep enough later," she says.

I sit up. "I don't go straight back to the front, Mother. I have to do four weeks at the training camp. I may come over from there one Sunday, perhaps."

She is silent. Then she asks gently: "Are you very much afraid?"

"No, Mother."

"I would like to tell you to be on your guard against the women out in France. They are no good."

Ah! Mother, Mother! You still think I am a child – why can I not put my head in your lap and weep? Why have I always to be strong and self-controlled? I would like to weep and be comforted, too, indeed I am little more than a child; in the wardrobe still hang my short, boy's trousers – it is such a little time ago, why is it over?

"Where we are there aren't any women, Mother," I say as calmly as I can.

"And be very careful at the front, Paul."

Ah, Mother, Mother! Why do I not take you in my arms and die with you? What poor wretches we are!

"Yes, Mother, I will."

"I will pray for you every day, Paul."

Ah! Mother, Mother! Let us rise up and go out, back through the

142

years, where the burden of all this misery lies on us no more, back to you and me alone, Mother!

"Perhaps you can get a job that is not so dangerous."

"Yes, Mother, perhaps I can get into the cook-house, that can easily be done."

"You do it then, and if the others say anything – "

"That won't worry me, Mother – "

She sighs. Her face is a white gleam in the darkness.

"Now you must go to sleep, Mother."

She does not reply. I get up and wrap my cover round her shoulders.

She supports herself on my arm, she is in pain. And so I take her to her room. I stay with her a little while.

"And you must get well again, Mother, before I come back."

"Yes, yes, my child."

"You ought not to send your things to me, Mother. We have plenty to eat out there. You can make much better use of them here."

How destitute she lies there in her bed, she, that loves me more than all the world. As I am about to leave, she says hastily: "I have two pairs of underpants for you. They are all wool. They will keep you warm. You must not forget to put them in your pack."

Ah! Mother! I know what these underpants have cost you in waiting, and walking, and begging! Ah! Mother, Mother! how can it be that I must part from you? Who else is there that has any claim on me but you? Here I sit and there you are lying, and we have so much to say, that we could never say it.

"Good-night, Mother."

"Good-night, my child."

The room is dark. I hear my mother's breathing, and the ticking of the clock. Outside the window the wind blows and the chestnut trees rustle.

On the landing I stumble over my pack which lies there already made up, because I have to leave early in the morning.

143

I bite into my pillow. I grasp the iron rods of my bed with my fists. I ought never to have come here. Out there I was indifferent and often hopeless; – I will never be able to be so again. I was a soldier, and now I am nothing but an agony for myself, for my mother, for everything that is so comfortless and without end.

I ought never to have come on leave.

Chapter Eight

I ALREADY KNOW the camp on the moors. It was here that Himmelstoss gave Tjaden his education. But now I know hardly anyone here; as ever, all is altered. There are only a few people that I have occasionally met before.

I go through the routine mechanically. In the evenings I generally go to the Soldiers' Home, where the newspapers are laid out, but which I do not read; still, there is a piano there that I am glad enough to play on. Two girls are in attendance, one of them is young.

The camp is surrounded with high barbed-wire fences. If we come back late from the Soldiers' Home we have to show passes. But those who are on good terms with the guard can get through, of course.

Between the junipers and the birch trees on the moor we practise company-drill each day. It is bearable if one expects nothing better. We advance at a run, fling ourselves down, and our panting breath moves the stalks of the grasses and the flowers of the heather to and fro. Looked at so closely one sees the fine sand is composed of millions of the tiniest pebbles as clear as if they had been made in a laboratory. It is strangely inviting to dig one's hands into it.

But most beautiful are the woods with their line of birch trees. Their colour changes with every minute. Now the stems gleam purest

144

white, and between them, airy and silken, hangs the pastel-green of the leaves; the next moment all changes to an opalescent blue, as the shivering breezes pass down from the heights and touch the green lightly away; and again in one place it deepens almost to black as a cloud passes over the sun. And this shadow moves like a ghost through the dim trunks and passes far out over the moor to the sky – then the birches stand out again like gay banners on white poles, with their red and gold patches of autumn-tinted leaves.

I often become so lost in the play of soft light and transparent shadow, that I almost fail to hear the commands. It is when one is alone that one begins to observe Nature and to love her. And here I have not much companionship, and do not even desire it. We are too little acquainted with one another to do more than joke a bit and play poker or nap in the evenings.

Alongside our camp is the big Russian prison camp. It is separated from us by a wire fence, but in spite of this the prisoners come across to us. They seem nervous and fearful, though most of them are big fellows with beards – they look like meek, scolded, St. Bernard dogs.

They slink about our camp and pick over the garbage tins. One can imagine what they find there. With us food is pretty scarce and none too good at that – turnips cut into six pieces and boiled in water, and unwashed carrot tops; – mouldy potatoes are tit-bits, and the chief luxury is a thin rice soup in which float little bits of beef-sinew, but these are cut up so small that they take a lot of finding.

Everything gets eaten, notwithstanding, and if ever anyone is so well off as not to want all his share, there are a dozen others standing by ready to relieve him of it. Only the dregs that the ladle cannot reach are tipped out and thrown into the garbage tins. Along with that sometimes go a few turnip peelings, mouldy bread crusts and all kinds of muck.

This thin, miserable, dirty garbage is the objective of the prisoners.

They pick it out of the stinking tins greedily and go off with it under their blouses.

It is strange to see these enemies of ours so close up. They have faces that make one think – honest peasant faces, broad foreheads, broad noses, broad mouths, broad hands, and thick hair.

They ought to be put to threshing, reaping, and apple picking. They look just as kindly as our own peasants in Friesland.

It is distressing to watch their movements, to see them begging for something to eat. They are all rather feeble, for they only get enough nourishment to keep them from starving. Ourselves we have not had sufficient to eat for long enough. They have dysentery; furtively many of them display the bloodstained tails of their shirts. Their backs, their necks are bent, their knees sag, their heads droop as they stretch out their hands and beg in the few words of German that they know – beg with those soft, deep, musical voices, that are like warm stoves and cosy rooms at home.

Some men there are who give them a kick, so that they fall over; — but those are not many. The majority do nothing to them, just ignore them. Occasionally, when they are too grovelling, it makes a man mad and then he kicks them. If only they would not look at one so — What great misery can be in two such small spots, no bigger than a man's thumb — in their eyes!

They come over to the camp in the evenings and trade. They exchange whatever they possess for bread. Often they have fair success, because they have very good boots and ours are bad. The leather of their knee boots is wonderfully soft, like suede. The peasants among us who get tit-bits sent from home can afford to trade. The price of a pair of boots is about two or three loaves of army bread, or a loaf of bread and a small, tough ham sausage.

But most of the Russians have long since parted with whatever things they had. Now they wear only the most pitiful clothing, and try to exchange little carvings and objects that they have made out of shell fragments and copper driving-bands. Of course, they don't get much for such things, though they may have taken immense pains with them – they go for a slice or two of bread. Our peasants are hard and cunning when they bargain. They hold the piece of bread or sausage right under the nose of the Russian till he grows pale with greed and his eyes bulge and then he will give anything for it. The peasants wrap up their booty with the utmost solemnity, and then get out their big pocket knives, and slowly and deliberately cut off a slice of bread for themselves from their supply and with every mouthful take a piece of the good, tough sausage and so reward themselves with a good feed. It is distressing to watch them take their afternoon meal thus; one would like to crack them over their thick pates. They rarely give anything away. How little we understand one another!

I am often on guard over the Russians. In the darkness one sees their forms move like sick storks, like great birds. They come close up to the wire fence and lean their faces against it; their fingers hook round the mesh. Often many stand side by side, and breathe the wind that comes down from the moors and the forest.

They rarely speak and then only a few words. They are more human and more brotherly towards one another, it seems to me, than we are. But perhaps that is merely because they feel themselves to be more unfortunate than us. Anyway the war is over so far as they are concerned. But to wait for dysentery is not much of a life either.

The Territorials who are in charge of them say that they were much more lively at first. They used to have intrigues among themselves, as always happens, and it would often come to blows and knives. But now they are quite apathetic, and listless.

They stand at the wire fence; sometimes one goes away and then another at once takes his place in the line. Most of them are silent; occasionally one begs a cigarette butt.

I see their dark forms, their beards move in the wind. I know nothing of them except that they are prisoners, and that is exactly what troubles me. Their life is obscure and guiltless; – if I could know more of them, what their names are, how they live, what they are waiting for, what are their burdens, then my emotion would have an object and might become sympathy. But as it is I perceive behind them only the suffering of the creature, the awful melancholy of life and the pitilessness of men.

A word of command has made these silent figures our enemies; a word of command might transform them into our friends. At some table a document is signed by some persons whom none of us knows, and then for years together that very crime on which formerly the world's condemnation and severest penalty fell becomes our highest aim. But who can draw such a distinction when he looks at these quiet men with their childlike faces and apostles' beards. Any non-commissioned officer is more of an enemy to a recruit, any schoolmaster to a pupil than they are to us. And yet we would shoot at them again and they at us if they were free.

I am frightened: I dare think this way no more. This way lies the abyss. It is not now the time; but I will not lose these thoughts, I will keep them, shut them away until the war is ended. My heart beats fast: is this the aim, the great, the sole aim, that I have thought of in the trenches, that I have looked for as the only possibility of existence after this annihilation of all human feeling; is this a task that will make life afterward worth these hideous years?

I take out my cigarettes, break each one in half and give them to the Russians. They bow to me and then they light the cigarettes. Now red points glow in every face. They comfort me; it looks as though there were little windows in dark village cottages saying that behind them are rooms full of peace.

The days go by. On a foggy morning another of the Russians is buried; almost every day one of them dies. I am on guard during the burial. The prisoners sing a chorale, they sing in parts, and it sounds almost as if there were no voices, but an organ far away on the moor.

The burial is quickly over.

In the evening they stand again at the wire fence and the wind comes down to them from the birch woods. The stars are cold.

I now know a few of those who speak a little German. There is a musician amongst them, he says he used to be a violinist in Berlin. When he hears that I can play the piano he fetches his violin and plays. The others sit down and lean their backs against the fence. He stands up and plays, sometimes he has that absent expression which violinists get when they close their eyes; or again he sways the instrument to the rhythm and smiles across to me.

He plays mostly folk-songs and the others hum with him. They are like a country of dark hills that sing far down under the ground. The sound of the violin stands like a slender girl above it and is clear and alone. The voices cease and the violin continues alone. In the night it is so thin it sounds frozen; one must stand close up; it would be much better in a room; – out here it makes a man grow sad.

Because I have already had a long leave I get none on Sundays. So the last Sunday before I go back to the front my father and eldest sister come over to see me. All day we sit in the Soldiers' Home. Where else could we go, we don't want to stay in the camp. About midday we go for a walk on the moors.

The hours are a torture; we do not know what to talk about, so we speak of my mother's illness. It is now definitely cancer, she is already

154

in the hospital and will be operated on shortly. The doctors hope she
will recover, but we have never heard of cancer being cured.

"Where is she then?" I ask.

"In the Luisa Hospital," says my father.

"In which class?"

"Third. We must wait till we know what the operation costs. She
wanted to be in the third herself. She said that then she would have
some company. And besides it is cheaper."

"So she is lying there with all those people. If only she could sleep
properly."

My father nods. His face is broken and full of furrows. My mother
has always been sickly; and though she has only gone to the hospital
when she has been compelled to, it has cost a great deal of money,
and my father's life has been practically given up to it.

"If only I knew how much the operation costs," says he.

"Have you not asked?"

"Not directly, I cannot do that – the surgeon might take it amiss
and that would not do, he must operate on Mother."

Yes, I think bitterly, that's how it is with us, and with all poor
people. They don't dare to ask the price, but worry themselves dreadfully beforehand about it; but the others, for whom it is not important,
they settle the price first as a matter of course. And the doctor does
not take it amiss from them.

"And the dressings afterwards are so expensive," says my father.

"Doesn't the Invalid's Fund pay anything toward it, then?" I ask.

"Mother has been ill too long."

"Have you any money at all?"

He shakes his head: "No, but I can do some overtime."

I know. He will stand at his desk folding and pasting and cutting
until twelve o'clock at night. At eight o'clock in the evening he will
eat some of the miserable rubbish they get in exchange for their food

tickets, then he will take a powder for his headache and work on.

In order to cheer him up a bit I tell him a few stories, soldiers' jokes, and the like, about generals and sergeant-majors.

Afterwards I accompany them both to the railway station. They give me a pot of jam and a bag of potato-cakes that my mother has made for me.

Then they go off and I return to the camp.

In the evening I spread the jam on the cakes and eat some. But I have no taste for them. So I go out to give them to the Russians. Then it occurs to me that my mother cooked them herself and that she was probably in pain as she stood before the hot stove. I put the bag back in my pack and take only two cakes to the Russians.

Chapter Nine

WE TRAVEL for several days. The first aeroplanes appear in the sky. We roll on past transport lines. Guns, guns. The light railway picks us up. I search for my regiment. No one knows exactly where it lies. Somewhere or other I put up for the night, somewhere or other I receive provisions and a few vague instructions. And so with my pack and my rifle I set out again on the way.

By the time I come up they are no longer in that devastated place. I hear we have become one of the flying divisions that are pushed in wherever it is hottest. That does not sound cheerful to me. They tell me of heavy losses that we have been having. I enquire after Kat and Albert. No one knows anything of them.

I search farther and wander about here and there; it is a wonderful feeling. One night and then another I camp out like a Red Indian.

Then at last I get some definite information, and by the afternoon I am able to report to the Orderly Room.

The sergeant-major detains me there. The company comes back in two days' time. There is no object in sending me up now.

"What was it like on leave?" he asks, "pretty good, eh?"

"In parts," I say.

"Yes," he sighs, "yes, if a man didn't have to come away again. The second half is always rather messed up by that."

I loaf around until the company comes back in the early morning, grey, dirty, soured, and gloomy. Then I jump up, push in amongst them, my eyes searching. There is Tjaden, there is Müller blowing his nose, and there are Kat and Kropp. We arrange our sacks of straw side by side. I have an uneasy conscience when I look at them, and yet without any good reason. Before we turn in I bring out the rest of the potato-cakes and jam so that they can have some too.

The two outer cakes are mouldy, still it is possible to eat them. I keep those for myself and give the fresh ones to Kat and Kropp.

Kat chews and says: "These are from your mother?"

I nod.

"Good," says he, "I can tell by the taste."

I could almost weep. I can hardly control myself any longer. But it will soon be all right again back here with Kat and Albert. This is where I belong.

"You've been lucky," whispers Kropp to me before we drop off to sleep, "they say we are going to Russia."

To Russia. It's not much of a war over there.

In the distance the front thunders. The walls of the hut rattle.

There's a great deal of polishing being done. We are inspected at every turn. Everything that is torn is exchanged for new. I score a spotless new tunic out of it and Kat, of course, an entire outfit. A rumour is

157

going round that there may be peace, but the other story is more likely – that we are bound for Russia. Still, what do we need new things for in Russia? At last it leaks out – the Kaiser is coming to review us. Hence all the inspections.

For eight whole days one would suppose we were in a base-camp, there is so much drill and fuss. Everyone is peevish and touchy, we do not take kindly to all this polishing, much less to parades. Such things exasperate a soldier more than the front-line.

At last the moment arrives. We stand up stiff and the Kaiser appears. We are curious to see what he looks like. He stalks along the line, and I am really rather disappointed; judging from his pictures I imagined him to be bigger and more powerfully built, and above all to have a thundering voice.

He distributes Iron Crosses and speaks to this man and to that. Then we march off.

Afterwards we discuss it. Tjaden says with astonishment:

"So that is the All-Highest! And everyone, bar nobody, has to stand up stiff in front of him!" He meditates: "Hindenburg too, he has to stand up stiff to him, eh?"

"Sure," says Kat.

Tjaden hasn't finished yet. He thinks for a while and then asks: "And would a king have to stand up stiff to an emperor?"

None of us is quite sure about it, but we don't suppose so. They are both so exalted that standing strictly to attention is probably not insisted on.

"What rot you do hatch out," says Kat. "The main point is that you have to stand stiff yourself."

But Tjaden is quite fascinated. His otherwise prosy fancy is blowing bubbles. "But look," he announces, "I simply can't believe that an emperor has to go to the latrine the same as I do."

"You can bet your boots on it."

158

"Four and a half-wit make seven," says Kat. "You've got a maggot in your brain, Tjaden, just you run along to the latrine quick, and get your head clear, so that you don't talk like a two-year-old."

Tjaden disappears.

"But what I would like to know," says Albert, "is whether there would not have been a war if the Kaiser had said No."

"I'm sure of this much," I interject, "he was against it from the first."

"Well, if not him alone, then perhaps if twenty or thirty people in the world had said No."

"That's probable," I agree, "but they damned well said Yes."

"It's queer, when one thinks about it," goes on Kropp, "we are here to protect our fatherland. And the French are over there to protect their fatherland. Now, who's in the right?"

"Perhaps both," say I, without believing it.

"Yes, well now," pursues Albert, and I see that he means to drive me into a corner, "but our professors and parsons and newspapers say that we are the only ones that are right, and let's hope so; – but the French professors and parsons and newspapers say that the right is on their side, what about that?"

"That I don't know," I say, "but whichever way it is there's war all the same and every month more countries coming in."

Tjaden reappears. He is still quite excited and again joins the conversation, wondering just how a war gets started.

"Mostly by one country badly offending another," answers Albert with a slight air of superiority.

Then Tjaden pretends to be obtuse. "A country? I don't follow. A mountain in Germany cannot offend a mountain in France. Or a river, or a wood, or a field of wheat."

"Are you really as stupid as that, or are you just pulling my leg?" growls Kropp. "I don't mean that at all. One people offends the other – "

"Then I haven't any business here at all," replies Tjaden. "I don't feel myself offended."

"Well, let me tell you," says Albert sourly, "it doesn't apply to tramps like you."

"Then I can be going home right away," retorts Tjaden, and we all laugh.

"Ach, man! he means the people as a whole, the State – " exclaims Müller.

"State, State" – Tjaden snaps his fingers contemptuously. "Gendarmes, police, taxes, that's your State; – if that's what you are talking about, no thank you."

"That's right," says Kat, "you've said something for once, Tjaden. State and home-country, there's a big difference."

"But they go together," insists Kropp, "without the State there wouldn't be any home-country."

"True, but just you consider, almost all of us are simple folk. And in France, too, the majority of men are labourers, workmen, or poor clerks. Now just why would a French blacksmith or a French shoe-maker want to attack us? No, it is merely the rulers. I had never seen a Frenchman before I came here, and it will be just the same with the majority of Frenchmen as regards us. They weren't asked about it any more than we were."

"Then what exactly is the war for?" asks Tjaden.

Kat shrugs his shoulders. "There must be some people to whom the war is useful."

"Well, I'm not one of them," grins Tjaden.

"Not you, nor anybody else here."

"Who are they then?" persists Tjaden. "It isn't any use to the Kaiser either. He has everything he can want already."

"I'm not so sure about that," contradicts Kat, "he has not had a war up till now. And every full-grown emperor requires at least one war, other-

160

wise he wouldn't become famous. You look in your school books."

"And generals too," adds Detering, "they become famous through war."

"Even more famous than emperors," adds Kat.

"There are other people back behind there who profit by the war, that's certain," growls Detering.

"I think it is more a kind of fever," says Albert. "No one in particular wants it, and then all at once there it is. We didn't want the war, the others say the same thing – and yet half the world is in it all the same."

"But there are more lies told by the other side than by us," say I; "just think of those pamphlets the prisoners have on them, where it says that we eat Belgian children. The fellows who write that ought to go and hang themselves. They are the real culprits."

Müller gets up. "Anyway, it is better that the war is here instead of in Germany. Just you take a look at the shell-holes."

"True," assents Tjaden, "but no war at all would be better still."

He is quite proud of himself because he has for once scored over us volunteers. And his opinion is quite typical here, one meets it time and again, and there is nothing with which one can properly counter it, because that is the limit of their comprehension of the factors involved. The national feeling of the soldier resolves itself into this – here he is. But that is the end of it; everything else from joining up onwards he criticizes from a practical point of view.

Albert lies down on the grass and growls angrily: "The best thing is not to talk about the rotten business."

"It won't make any difference, that's sure," agrees Kat.

As for the windfall, we have to return almost all the new things and take back our old rags again. The good ones were merely for the inspection.

Instead of going to Russia, we go up the line again. On the way we pass through a devastated wood with the tree trunks shattered and the ground ploughed up.

At several places there are tremendous craters. "Great guns, something's hit that," I say to Kat.

"Trench mortars," he replies, and then points up at one of the trees.

In the branches dead men are hanging. A naked soldier is squatting in the fork of a tree, he still has his helmet on, otherwise he is entirely unclad. There is only half of him sitting up there, the top half, the legs are missing.

"What can that mean?" I ask.

"He's been blown out of his clothes," mutters Tjaden.

"It's funny," says Kat, "we have seen that a couple of times now. If a mortar gets you it blows you almost clean out of your clothes. It's the concussion that does it."

I search around. And so it is. Here hang bits of uniform, and somewhere else is plastered a bloody mess that was once a human limb. Over there lies a body with nothing but a piece of the underpants on one leg and the collar of the tunic around its neck. Otherwise it is naked and the clothes are hanging up in the tree. Both arms are missing as though they had been pulled out. I discover one of them twenty yards off in a shrub.

The dead man lies on his face. There, where the arm wounds are,

162

the earth is black with blood. Underfoot the leaves are scratched up as though the man had been kicking.

"That's no joke, Kat," say I.

"No more is a shell splinter in the belly," he replies, shrugging his shoulders.

"But don't get tender-hearted," says Tjaden.

All this can only have happened a little while ago, the blood is still fresh. As everybody we see there is dead we do not waste any more time, but report the affair at the next stretcher-bearers' post. After all it is not our business to take these stretcher-bearers' jobs away from them.

A patrol has to be sent out to discover just how far the enemy position is advanced. Since my leave I feel a certain strange attachment to the other fellows, and so I volunteer to go with them. We agree on a plan, slip out through the wire and then divide and creep forward separately. After a while I find a shallow shell-hole and crawl into it. From here I peer forward.

There is moderate machine-gun fire. It sweeps across from all directions, not very heavy, but always sufficient to make one keep down.

A parachute star-shell opens out. The ground lies stark in the pale light, and then the darkness shuts down again blacker than ever. In the trenches we were told there were black troops in front of us. That is nasty, it is hard to see them; they are very good at patrolling, too. And oddly enough they are often quite stupid; for instance, both Kat and Kropp were once able to shoot down a black enemy patrol because the fellows in their enthusiasm for cigarettes smoked while they were creeping about. Kat and Albert had simply to aim at the glowing ends of the cigarettes.

A bomb or something lands close beside me. I have not heard it coming and am terrified. At the same moment a senseless fear takes hold on me. Here I am alone and almost helpless in the dark – perhaps two other eyes have been watching me for a long while from another shell-hole in front of me, and a bomb lies ready to blow me to pieces. I try to pull myself together. It is not my first patrol and not a particularly risky one. But it is the first since my leave, and besides, the lie of the land is still rather strange to me.

I tell myself that my alarm is absurd, that there is probably nothing

164

at all there in the darkness watching me, because otherwise the missile would not have landed so flat.

It is in vain. In whirling confusion my thoughts hum in my brain − I hear the warning voice of my mother, I see the Russians with the flowing beards leaning against the wire fence, I have a bright picture of a canteen with stools, of a cinema in Valenciennes; tormented, terrified, in my imagination I see the grey, impalpable muzzle of a rifle which moves noiselessly before me whichever way I try to turn my head. The sweat breaks out from every pore.

I still continue to lie in my shallow bowl. I look at the time; only a few minutes have passed. My forehead is wet, the sockets of my eyes are damp, my hands tremble, and I am panting softly. It is nothing but an awful spasm of fear, a simple animal fear of poking out my head and crawling on farther.

All my efforts subside like froth into the one desire to be able just to stay lying there. My limbs are glued to the earth. I make a vain attempt; − they refuse to come away. I press myself down on the earth, I cannot go forward, I make up my mind to stay lying there.

But immediately the wave floods over me anew, a mingled sense of shame, of remorse, and yet at the same time of security. I raise myself up a little to take a look around.

My eyes burn with staring into the dark. A star-shell goes up; − I duck down again.

I wage a wild and senseless fight, I want to get out of the hollow and yet slide back into it again, I say: "You must, it is your comrades, it is not any idiotic command," and again: "What does it matter to me, I have only one life to lose − "

That is the result of all this leave, I reproach myself bitterly. But I cannot convince myself, I become terribly faint. I raise myself slowly and reach forward with my arms, dragging my body after me and then lie on the edge of the shell-hole, half in and half out.

There I hear sounds and drop back. Suspicious sounds can be detected clearly despite the noise of the artillery-fire. I listen; the sound is behind me. They are our people moving along the trench. Now I hear muffled voices. To judge by the tone that might be Kat talking.

At once a new warmth flows through me. These voices, these few quiet words, these footsteps in the trench behind me recall me at a bound from the terrible loneliness and fear of death by which I had been almost destroyed. They are more to me than life, these voices, they are more than motherliness and more than fear; they are the strongest, most comforting thing there is anywhere: they are the voices of my comrades.

I am no longer a shuddering speck of existence, alone in the darkness; – I belong to them and they to me, we all share the same fear and the same life, we are nearer than lovers, in a simpler, a harder way; I could bury my face in them, in these voices, these words that have saved me and will stand by me.

Cautiously I glide out over the edge and snake my way forward. I shuffle along on all fours a bit farther, I keep track of my bearings, look around me and observe the distribution of the gun-fire so as to be able to find my way back. Then I try to get in touch with the others.

I am still afraid, but it is an intelligent fear, an extraordinarily heightened caution. The night is windy and shadows flit hither and thither in the flicker of the gun-fire. It reveals too little and too much. Often I peer ahead, but always for nothing. Thus I advance a long way and then turn back in a wide curve. I have not established touch with the others. Every yard nearer our trench fills me with confidence; – and with haste, too. It would be bad to get lost now.

Then a new fear lays hold of me. I can no longer remember the direction. Quiet, I squat in a shell-hole and try to locate myself. More

166

than once it has happened that some fellow has jumped joyfully into a trench only then to discover that it was the wrong one.

After a little time I listen again, but still I am not sure. The confusion of shell-holes now seems so bewildering that I can no longer tell in my agitation which way I should go. Perhaps I am crawling parallel to the lines, and that might go on for ever. So I crawl round once again in a wide curve.

These damned rockets! They seem to burn for an hour, and a man cannot make the least movement without bringing the bullets whistling round.

But there is nothing for it, I must get out. Falteringly I work my way farther, I move off over the ground like a crab and rip my hands sorely on the jagged splinters, as sharp as razor blades. Often I think that the sky is becoming lighter on the horizon, but it may be merely my imagination. Then gradually I realize that to crawl in the right direction is a matter of life or death.

A shell crashes. Almost immediately two others. And then it begins in earnest. A bombardment. Machine-guns rattle. Now there is nothing for it but to stay lying low. Apparently an attack is coming. Everywhere the rockets shoot up. Unceasing.

I lie huddled in a large shell-hole, my legs in the water up to the belly. When the attack starts I will let myself fall into the water, with my face as deep in the mud as I can keep it without suffocating. I must pretend to be dead.

Suddenly I hear the barrage lift. At once I slip down into the water, my helmet on the nape of my neck and my mouth just clear so that I can get a breath of air.

I lie motionless; – somewhere something clanks, it stamps and stumbles nearer – all my nerves become taut and icy. It clatters over me and away, the first wave has passed. I have but this one shattering thought: What will you do if someone jumps into your shell-hole? –

167

Swiftly I pull out my little dagger, grasp it fast and bury it in my hand once again under the mud. If anyone jumps in here I will go for him; it hammers in my forehead; at once, stab him clean through the throat, so that he cannot call out; that's the only way; he will be just as frightened as I am, when in terror we fall upon one another, then I must be first.

Now our batteries are firing. A shell lands near me. That makes me savage with fury, all it needs now is to be killed by our own shells; I curse and grind my teeth in the mud; it is a raving frenzy; in the end all I can do is groan and pray.

The crash of the shells bursts in my ears. If our fellows make a counter-raid I will be saved. I press my head against the earth and listen to the muffled thunder, like the explosions of quarrying – and raise it again to listen for the sounds on top.

The machine-guns rattle. I know our barbed-wire entanglements are strong and almost undamaged; – parts of them are charged with a powerful electric current. The rifle-fire increases. They have not broken through; they have to retreat.

I sink down again, huddled, strained to the uttermost. The banging, the creeping, the clanging becomes audible. One single cry yelling amongst it all. They are raked with fire, the attack is repulsed.

Already it has become somewhat lighter. Steps hasten over me. The first. Gone. Again, another. The rattle of machine-guns becomes an unbroken chain. Just as I am about to turn round a little, something heavy stumbles, and with a crash a body falls over me into the shell-hole, slips down, and lies across me –

I do not think at all, I make no decision – I strike madly home, and feel only how the body suddenly convulses, then becomes limp, and collapses. When I recover myself, my hand is sticky and wet.

The man gurgles. It sounds to me as though he bellows, every gasp-

168

ing breath is like a cry, a thunder – but it is only my heart pounding.
I want to stop his mouth, stuff it with earth, stab him again, he must
be quiet, he is betraying me; now at last I regain control of myself,
but have suddenly become so feeble that I cannot any more lift my
hand against him.

So I crawl away to the farthest corner and stay there, my eyes glued
on him, my hand grasping the knife – ready, if he stirs, to spring at
him again. But he won't do so any more, I can hear that already in
his gurgling.

I can see him indistinctly. I have but one desire, to get away. If it
is not soon it will be too light; it will be difficult enough now. Then
as I try to raise up my head I see it is impossible already. The machine-
gun fire so sweeps the ground that I would be shot through and
through before I could make one jump.

I test it once with my helmet, which I take off and hold up to find out the level of the shots. The next moment it is knocked out of my hand by a bullet. The fire is sweeping very low over the ground. I am not far enough from the enemy line to escape being picked off by one of the snipers if I attempt to get away.

The light increases. Burning I wait for our attack. My hands are white at the knuckles, I clench them so tightly in my longing for the fire to cease so that my comrades may come.

Minute after minute trickles away. I dare not look again at the dark figure in the shell-hole. With an effort I look past it and wait, wait. The bullets hiss, they make a steel net, never ceasing, never ceasing.

Then I notice my bloody hand and suddenly feel nauseated. I take some earth and rub the skin with it, now my hand is muddy and the blood cannot be seen any more.

The fire does not diminish. It is equally heavy from both sides. Our fellows have probably given me up for lost long ago.

170

It is early morning, clear and grey. The gurgling continues, I stop my ears, but soon take my fingers away again, because then I cannot hear the other sound.

The figure opposite me moves. I shrink together and involuntarily look at it. Then my eyes remain glued to it. A man with a small pointed beard lies there, his head is fallen to one side, one arm is half-bent, his head rests helplessly upon it. The other hand lies on his chest, it is bloody.

He is dead, I say to myself, he must be dead, he doesn't feel anything any more; it is only the body that is gurgling there. Then the head tries to raise itself, for a moment the groaning becomes louder, his forehead sinks back upon his arm. The man is not dead, he is dying, but he is not dead. I drag myself toward him, hesitate, support myself on my hands, creep a bit farther, wait, again a terrible journey of three yards, a long, a terrible journey. At last I am beside him.

Then he opens his eyes. He must have heard me and gazes at me with a look of utter terror. The body lies still, but in the eyes there is such an extraordinary expression of flight that for a moment I think they have power enough to carry the body off with them. Hundreds of miles away with one bound. The body is still, perfectly still, without sound, the gurgle has ceased, but the eyes cry out, yell, all the life is gathered together in them for one tremendous effort to flee, gathered together there in a dreadful terror of death, of me.

My legs give way and I drop on my elbows. "No, no," I whisper.

The eyes follow me. I am powerless to move so long as they are there.

Then his hand slips slowly from his breast, only a little bit, it sinks just a few inches, but this movement breaks the power of the eyes. I bend forward, shake my head and whisper: "No, no, no." I raise one hand, I must show him that I want to help him, I stroke his forehead.

The eyes shrink back as the hand comes, then they lose their stare, the eyelids droop lower, the tension is past. I open his collar and place his head more comfortably upright.

His mouth stands half open, it tries to form words. The lips are dry. My water bottle is not there. I have not brought it with me. But there is water in the mud, down at the bottom of the crater. I climb down, take out my handkerchief, spread it out, push it under and scoop up the yellow water that strains through into the hollow of my hand.

172

He gulps it down. I fetch some more. Then I unbutton his tunic in order to bandage him if it is possible. In any case I must do it, so that if the fellows over there capture me they will see that I wanted to help him, and so will not shoot me. He tries to resist, but his hand is too feeble. The shirt is stuck and will not come away, it is buttoned at the back. So there is nothing for it but to cut it off.

I look for the knife and find it again. But when I begin to cut the shirt the eyes open once more and the cry is in them again and the demented expression, so that I must close them, press them shut and whisper: "I want to help you, Comrade, *camerade, camerade, camerade* – " eagerly repeating the word, to make him understand.

There are three stabs. My field dressing covers them, the blood runs out under it, I press it tighter; there; he groans.

That is all I can do. Now we must wait, wait.

These hours. . . . The gurgling starts again – but how slowly a man dies! For this I know – he cannot be saved. Indeed, I have tried to tell myself that he will be, but at noon this pretence breaks down and melts before his groans. If only I had not lost my revolver crawling about, I would shoot him. Stab him I cannot.

By noon I am groping on the outer limits of reason. Hunger devours me, I could almost weep for something to eat, I cannot struggle against it. Again and again I fetch water for the dying man and drink some myself.

This is the first man I have killed with my hands, whom I can see close at hand, whose death is my doing. Kat and Kropp and Müller have experienced it already, when they have hit someone; it happens to many, in hand-to-hand fighting especially –

But every gasp lays my heart bare. This dying man has time with him, he has an invisible dagger with which he stabs me: Time and my thoughts.

I would give much if he would but stay alive. It is hard to lie here and to have to see and hear him.

In the afternoon, about three, he is dead.

I breathe freely again. But only for a short time. Soon the silence is more unbearable than the groans. I wish the gurgling were there again, gasping, hoarse, now whistling softly and again hoarse and loud.

It is mad, what I do. But I must do something. I prop the dead man up again so that he lies comfortably although he feels nothing any more. I close his eyes. They are brown, his hair is black and a bit curly at the sides.

The mouth is full and soft beneath his moustache; the nose is slightly arched, the skin brownish; it is now not so pale as it was before, when he was still alive. For a moment the face seems almost healthy; — then it collapses suddenly into the strange face of the dead that I have so often seen, strange faces, all alike.

No doubt his wife still thinks of him; she does not know what has happened. He looks as if he would often have written to her; — she will still be getting mail from him — To-morrow, in a week's time — perhaps even a stray letter a month hence. She will read it, and in it he will be speaking to her.

My state is getting worse, I can no longer control my thoughts. What would his wife look like? Like the little brunette on the other side of the canal? Does she belong to me now? Perhaps by this act she becomes mine. I wish Kantorek were sitting here beside me. If my mother could see me — The dead man might have had thirty more years of life if only I had impressed the way back to our trench more sharply on my memory. If only he had run two yards farther to the left, he might now be sitting in the trench over there and writing a fresh letter to his wife.

But I will get no further that way; for that is the fate of all of us: if Kemmerich's leg had been six inches to the right; if Haie Westhus had bent his back three inches further forward —

174

The silence spreads. I talk and must talk. So I speak to him and say to him: "Comrade, I did not want to kill you. If you jumped in here again, I would not do it, if you would be sensible too. But you were only an idea to me before, an abstraction that lived in my mind and called forth its appropriate response. It was that abstraction I stabbed. But now, for the first time, I see you are a man like me. I thought of your hand-grenades, of your bayonet, of your rifle; now I see your wife and your face and our fellowship. Forgive me, comrade. We always see it too late. Why do they never tell us that you are just poor devils like us, that your mothers are just as anxious as ours, and that we have the same fear of death, and the same dying and the same agony — Forgive me, comrade; how could you be my enemy? If we threw away these rifles and this uniform you could be my brother just like Kat and Albert. Take twenty years of my life, comrade, and stand up — take more, for I do not know what I can even attempt to do with it now."

It is quiet, the front is still except for the crackle of rifle-fire. The bullets rain over, they are not fired haphazard, but shrewdly aimed from all sides. I cannot get out.

"I will write to your wife," I say hastily to the dead man, "I will write to her, she must hear it from me, I will tell her everything I have told you, she shall not suffer, I will help her, and your parents too, and your child — "

His tunic is half open. The pocketbook is easy to find. But I hesitate to open it. In it is the book with his name. So long as I do not know his name perhaps I may still forget him, time will obliterate it, this picture. But his name, it is a nail that will be hammered into me and never come out again. It has the power to recall this for ever, it will always come back and stand before me.

Irresolutely I take the wallet in my hand. It slips out of my hand and falls open. Some pictures and letters drop out. I gather them up and want to put them back again, but the strain I am under, the uncertainty, the hunger, the danger, these hours with the dead man have confused me, I want to hasten the relief, to intensify and to end the torture, as one strikes an unendurably painful hand against the trunk of a tree, regardless of everything.

There are portraits of a woman and a little girl, small amateur photographs taken against an ivy-clad wall. Along with them are letters. I take them out and try to read them. Most of it I do not understand, it is so hard to decipher and I know scarcely any French. But each word I translate pierces me like a shot in the chest; – like a stab in the chest.

My brain is taxed beyond endurance. But I realize this much, that I will never dare to write to these people as I intended. Impossible. I look at the portraits once more; they are clearly not rich people. I might send them money anonymously if I earn anything later on. I seize upon that, it is at least something to hold on to. This dead man is bound up with my life, therefore I must do everything, promise everything, in order to save myself; I swear blindly that I mean to live only for his sake and his family, with wet lips I try to placate him – and deep down in me lies the hope that I may buy myself off in this way and perhaps even yet get out of this; it is a little stratagem: if only I am allowed to escape, then I will see to it. So I open the book and read slowly: – Gérard Duval, compositor.

With the dead man's pencil I write the address on an envelope, then swiftly thrust everything back into his tunic.

I have killed the printer, Gérard Duval. I must be a printer, I think confusedly, be a printer, printer –

By afternoon I am calmer. My fear was groundless. The name troubles me no more. The madness passes. "Comrade," I say to the dead man, but I say it calmly, "to-day you, to-morrow me. But if I come out of

176

it, comrade, I will fight against this, that has struck us both down; from you, taken life – and from me – ? Life also. I promise you, comrade. It shall never happen again."

The sun strikes low. I am stupefied with exhaustion and hunger. Yesterday is like a fog to me, there is no hope of getting out of this yet. I fall into a doze and do not at first realize that evening is approaching. The twilight comes. It seems to me to come quickly now. One hour more. If it were summer, it would be three hours more. One hour more.

Now suddenly I begin to tremble; something might happen in the interval. I think no more of the dead man, he is of no consequence to me now. With one bound the lust to live flares up again and everything that has filled my thoughts goes down before it. Now, merely to avert any ill-luck, I babble mechanically: "I will fulfil everything, fulfil everything I have promised you – " but already I know that I shall not do so.

Suddenly it occurs to me that my own comrades may fire on me as I creep up; they do not know I am coming. I will call out as soon as I can so that they will recognize me. I will stay lying in front of the trench until they answer me.

The first star. The front remains quiet. I breathe deeply and talk to myself in my excitement: "No foolishness now, Paul – quiet, Paul, quiet – then you will be saved, Paul." When I use my Christian name, it works as though someone else spoke to me, it has more power.

The darkness grows. My excitement subsides, I wait cautiously until the first rocket goes up. Then I crawl out of the shell-hole. I have forgotten the dead man. Before me lies the oncoming night and the pale gleaming field. I fix my eye on a shell-hole; the moment the light dies I scurry over into it, grope farther, spring into the next, duck down, scramble onward.

I come nearer. There, by the light of a rocket I see something move

177

in the wire, then it stiffens and lies still. Next time I see it again, yes, they are men from our trench. But I am suspicious until I recognize our helmets. Then I call. And immediately an answer rings out, my name: "Paul — Paul — "

I call again in answer. It is Kat and Albert who have come out with a stretcher to look for me.

"Are you wounded?"

"No, no — "

We drop into the trench. I ask for something to eat and wolf it down. Müller gives me a cigarette. In a few words I tell what happened. There is nothing new about it; it happens quite often. The night attack is the only unusual feature of the business. In Russia Kat once lay for two days behind the enemy lines before he could make his way back.

I do not mention the dead printer.

But by next morning I can keep it to myself no longer. I must tell Kat and Albert. They both try to calm me. "You can't do anything about it. What else could you have done? That is what you are here for."

I listen to them and feel comforted, reassured by their presence. It was mere drivelling nonsense that I talked out there in the shell-hole.

"Look there for instance," points Kat.

On the fire-step stand some snipers. They rest their rifles with telescopic sights on the parapet and watch the enemy front. Once and again a shot cracks out.

Then we hear the cry: "That's found a billet!" "Did you see how he leapt in the air?" Sergeant Oellrich turns round proudly and scores his points. He heads the shooting list for to-day with three unquestionable hits.

"What do you say to that?" asks Kat.

I nod.

178

"If he keeps that up he will get a little coloured bird for his button-hole by this evening," says Albert.

"Or rather he will soon be made acting-sergeant-major," says Kat.

We look at one another. "I would not do it," I say.

"All the same," says Kat, "it's very good for you to see it just now."

Sergeant Oellrich returns to the fire-step. The muzzle of his rifle searches to and fro.

"You don't need to lose any more sleep over your affair," nods Albert.

And now I hardly understand it myself any more.

"It was only because I had to lie there with him so long," I say. "After all, war is war."

Oellrich's rifle cracks out sharp and dry.

Chapter Ten

WE HAVE DROPPED IN for a good job. Eight of us have to guard a village that has been abandoned because it is being shelled too heavily.

In particular we have to watch the supply dump as that is not yet empty. We are supposed to provision ourselves from the same store. We are just the right people for that – Kat, Albert, Müller, Tjaden, Detering, our whole gang is there. Haie is dead, though. But we are mighty lucky all the same, all the other squads have had more casualties than we have.

We select, as a dug-out, a reinforced concrete cellar into which steps lead down from above. The entrance is protected by a separate concrete wall.

Now we develop an immense industry. This is an opportunity not

179

only to stretch one's legs, but to stretch one's soul also. We make the best use of such opportunities. The war is too desperate to allow us to be sentimental for long. That is only possible so long as things are not going too badly. After all, we cannot afford to be anything but matter-of-fact. So matter-of-fact, indeed, that I often shudder when a thought from the days before the war comes momentarily into my head. But it does not stay long.

We have to take things as lightly as we can, so we make the most of every opportunity, and nonsense stands stark and immediate beside horror. It cannot be otherwise, that is how we hearten ourselves. So we zealously set to work to create an idyll – an idyll of eating and sleeping, of course.

The floor is first covered with mattresses which we haul in from the houses. Even a soldier's behind likes to sit soft. Only in the middle of the floor is there any clear space. Then we furnish ourselves with blankets and eiderdowns, luxurious soft affairs. There is plenty of everything to be had in the town. Albert and I find a mahogany bed which can be taken to pieces, with a sky of blue silk and a lace coverlet. We sweat like monkeys moving it in, but a man cannot let a thing like that slip, and it would certainly be shot to pieces in a day or two.

Kat and I do a little patrolling through the houses. In very short time we have collected a dozen eggs and two pounds of fairly fresh butter. Suddenly there is a crash in the drawing-room, and an iron stove hurtles through the wall past us and on, a yard from us out through the wall behind. Two holes. It comes from the house opposite where a shell has just landed. "The swine," grimaces Kat, and we continue our search. All at once we prick up our ears, hurry across, and suddenly stand petrified – there running up and down in a little sty are two live sucking pigs. We rub our eyes and look once again to make certain. Yes, they are still there. We seize hold of them – no doubt about it, two real young pigs.

180

This will make a grand feed. About twenty yards from our dug-out there is a small house that was used as an officers' billet. In the kitchen is an immense fireplace with two ranges, pots, pans, and kettles – everything, even to a stack of small chopped wood in an outhouse – a regular cook's paradise.

Two of our fellows have been out in the fields all the morning hunting for potatoes, carrots, and green peas. We are quite uppish and sniff at the tinned stuff in the supply dump, we want fresh vegetables. In the dining-room there are already two heads of cauliflower.

The sucking pigs are slaughtered. Kat sees to them. We want to make potato-cakes to go with the roast. But we cannot find a grater for the potatoes. However, that difficulty is soon got over. With a nail we punch a lot of holes in a pot lid and there we have a grater. Three fellows put on thick gloves to protect their fingers against the grater, two others peel the potatoes, and the business gets going.

Kat samples the sucking pigs, the carrots, the peas, and the cauliflower. He even mixes a white sauce for the cauliflower. I fry the pancakes, four at a time. After ten minutes I get the knack of tossing the pan so that the pancakes which are done on the one side sail up, turn in the air and are caught again as they come down. The sucking pigs are baked whole. We all stand round them as before an altar.

In the meantime we receive visitors, a couple of wireless-men, who are generously invited to the feed. They sit in the living-room where there is a piano. One of them plays, the other sings "An der Weser." He sings feelingly, but with a rather Saxon accent. All the same it moves us as we stand at the fireplace preparing the good things.

Then we begin to realize that we are in for trouble. The observation balloons have spotted the smoke from our chimney, and the shells start to drop on us. They are those damned spraying little daisy-cutters that make only a small hole and scatter widely close to the ground. They keep dropping closer and closer all round us; still we cannot leave the grub in the lurch. A couple of splinters whizz through the top of the kitchen window. The roast is already cooked. But frying the pancakes is getting difficult. The explosions come so fast that the splinters strike oftener and oftener against the wall of the house and sweep in through the window. Whenever I hear a shell coming I drop down on one knee with the pan and the pancakes, and duck behind the wall of the window. Immediately afterwards I am up again and going on with the frying.

The Saxons stop singing – a fragment has smashed into the piano. At last everything is ready and we organize the transport of it back to the dug-out. After the next explosion two men dash across the fifty yards to the dug-out with the pots of vegetables. We see them disappear.

The next shot. Everyone ducks and then two more trot off, each with a big can of finest grade coffee, and reach the dug-out before the next explosion.

Then Kat and Kropp seize the masterpiece – the big dish with the brown, roasted sucking pigs. A screech, a knee bend, and away they race over the fifty yards of open country.

I stay to finish frying my last four pancakes; twice I have to drop on the floor; – after all, it means four pancakes more, and they are my favourite dish.

Then I grab the plate with the great pile of cakes and squeeze myself behind the house door. A hiss, a crash, and I gallop off with the plate clamped against my chest with both hands. I am almost in, I run like a deer, sweep round the wall, fragments clatter against the concrete, I tumble down the cellar steps, my elbows are skinned, but I have not lost a single pancake, nor even broken the plate.

About two o'clock we start the meal. It lasts till six. We drink coffee until half-past seven – officers' coffee from the supply dump – and smoke officers' cigars and cigarettes – also from the supply dump.

182

Punctually at half-past seven we begin the evening meal. About ten o'clock we throw the bones of the sucking pigs outside the door. Then there is cognac and rum – also from the blessed supply dump – and once again long, fat cigars with belly-bands. Tjaden suggests that it lacks only one thing: Girls from an officers' brothel.

Late in the evening we hear mewing. A little grey cat sits in the entrance. We entice it in and give it something to eat. And that wakes up our own appetites once more. Still chewing, we lie down to sleep. But the night is bad. We have eaten too much fat. Fresh baby pig is very griping to the bowels. There is an everlasting coming and going in the dug-out.

Burning houses stand out like torches against the night. Shells lumber across and crash down. Munition columns tear along the street. On one side the supply dump has been ripped open. In spite of all the flying fragments the drivers of the munition columns pour in like a swarm of bees and pounce on the bread. We let them have their own way. If we said anything it would only mean a good hiding for us. So we go differently about it. We explain that we are the guard and so know our way about, we get hold of the tinned stuff and exchange it for things we are short of. What does it matter anyhow – in a while it will all be blown to pieces. For ourselves we take some chocolate from the depot and eat it in slabs. Kat says it is good for loose bowels.

Almost a fortnight passes thus in eating, drinking, and roaming about. No one disturbs us. The town gradually vanishes under the shells and we lead a charmed life. So long as any part of the supply dump still stands we don't worry, we desire nothing better than to stay here till the end of the war.

Tjaden has become so fastidious that he only half smokes his cigars. With his nose in the air he explains to us that he was brought up that way. And Kat is most cheerful. In the morning his first call is: "Emil, bring in the caviare and coffee." We put on extraordinary airs, every man treats the other as his valet, and gives him orders insolently. "There is something itching under my foot; Kropp, my man, catch that louse at once," says Leer, poking out his leg at him like a ballet girl, and Albert drags him up the stairs by the foot. "Tjaden!" – "What?" – "Stand at ease, Tjaden; and what's more, don't say 'What,' say 'Yes, Sir,' – now: Tjaden!" Tjaden retorts in the well-known phrase from Goethe's "Götz von Berlichingen," with which he is always very free.

After eight more days we receive orders to go back. The palmy days are over. Two big motor lorries take us away. They are stacked high with planks. Nevertheless, Albert and I erect on top our four-poster bed complete with blue silk canopy, mattress, and two lace coverlets. And behind it at the head is stowed a bag full of choice edibles. We often dip into it, and the tough ham sausages, the tins of liver sausages, the conserves, the boxes of cigarettes rejoice our hearts. Each man has a bag to himself.

Kropp and I have rescued two big red armchairs as well. They stand inside the bed, and we sprawl back in them as in a theatre box. Above us swells the silken cover like a baldaquin. Each man has a long cigar in his mouth. And thus from aloft we survey the scene.

Between us stands a parrot-cage that we found for the cat. She is coming with us, and lies in the cage before her saucer of meat, and purrs.

Slowly the lorries roll down the road. We sing. Behind us the shells are sending up fountains from the now utterly abandoned town.

A few days later we are sent out to evacuate a village. On the way we meet the fleeing inhabitants trundling their goods and chattels along with them in wheelbarrows, perambulators, and on their backs. Their figures are bent, their faces full of grief, despair, haste, and resignation. The children hold on to their mothers' hands, and often an older girl leads the little ones who stumble onward and are for ever looking back. A few carry miserable-looking dolls. All are silent as they pass us by.

We are marching in column; the French do not fire on a town in which there are still inhabitants. But a few minutes later the air screams, the earth heaves, cries ring out; a shell has smashed into the rear squad. We scatter and fling ourselves down on the ground, but at that moment I feel the instinctive alertness leave me which

185

hitherto has always made me do unconsciously the right thing under fire; the thought leaps up with a terrible, throttling fear: "You are lost" – and the next moment a blow sweeps like a whip over my left leg. I hear Albert cry out; he is beside me.

"Quick, up, Albert!" I yell, for we are lying unsheltered in the open field.

He staggers up and runs. I keep beside him. We have to get over a hedge; it is higher than we are. Kropp seizes a branch, I heave him up by the leg, he cries out, I give him a swing and he flies over. With one leap I follow him and fall into a ditch that lies behind the hedge.

Our faces are smothered with duck-weed and mud, but the cover is good. So we wade in up to our necks. Whenever a shell whistles we duck our heads under the water. After we have done this a dozen times, I am exhausted.

"Let's get away, or I'll fall in and drown," groans Albert.

"Where has it got you?" I ask him.

"In the knee, I think."

"Can you run?"

"I think – "

"Then out!"

We make for the ditch beside the road, and stooping, run along it. The shelling follows us. The road leads toward the munition dump. If that goes up there won't be a man of us with his head left on his shoulders. So we change our plan and run diagonally across country.

Albert begins to drag. "You go, I'll come on after," he says, and throws himself down.

I seize him by the arm and shake him. "Up, Albert, if you once lie down you'll never get any farther. Quick, I'll hold you up."

At last we reach a small dug-out. Kropp pitches in and I bandage him up. The shot is just a little above his knee. Then I take a look at myself. My trousers are bloody and my arm, too. Albert binds up my

186

wounds with his field dressing. Already he is no longer able to move his leg, and we both wonder how we managed to get this far. Fear alone made it possible; we would have run even if our feet had been shot off; – we would have run on the stumps.

I can still crawl a little. I call out to a passing ambulance wagon which picks us up. It is full of wounded. There is an army medical lance-corporal with it who sticks an anti-tetanus needle into our chests.

At the dressing-station we arrange matters so that we lie side by side. They give us a thin soup which we spoon down greedily and scornfully, because we are accustomed to better times but are hungry all the same.

"Now for home, Albert," I say.

"Let's hope so," he replies, "I only wish I knew what I've got."

The pain increases. The bandages burn like fire. We drink and drink, one glass of water after another.

"How far above the knee am I hit?" asks Kropp.

"At least four inches, Albert," I answer. Actually it is perhaps one.

"I've made up my mind," he says after a while, "if they take off my leg, I'll put an end to it. I won't go through life as a cripple."

So we lie there with our thoughts and wait.

In the evening we are hauled onto the chopping-block. I am frightened and think quickly what I ought to do; for everyone knows that the surgeons in the dressing-stations amputate on the slightest provocation. Under the great pressure of business that is much simpler than complicated patching. I think of Kemmerich. Whatever happens I will not let them chloroform me, even if I have to crack a couple of their skulls.

It is all right. The surgeon pokes around in the wound and a blackness comes before my eyes. "Don't carry on so," he says gruffly, and hacks away. The instruments gleam in the bright light like malevo-

187

lent animals. The pain is insufferable. Two orderlies hold my arms fast, but I break loose from one of them and try to crash into the surgeon's spectacles just as he notices and springs back. "Chloroform the scoundrel," he roars madly.

Then I become quiet. "Pardon me, Herr Doctor, I will keep still, but do not chloroform me."

"Well now," he cackles and takes up his instrument again. He is a fair fellow, not more than thirty years old, with scars and disgusting gold spectacles. Now I see that he is tormenting me, he is merely raking about in the wound and looking up surreptitiously at me over his glasses. My hands squeeze around the grips, I'll kick the bucket before he will get a squeak out of me.

He has fished out a piece of shell and tosses it to me. Apparently he is pleased at my self-control, for he seems to be more considerate of me now and says: "To-morrow you'll be off home." Then I am put in plaster. When I am back again with Kropp I tell him that apparently a hospital train comes in to-morrow morning.

"We must work the army medical sergeant-major so that we can keep together, Albert."

I manage to slip the sergeant-major two of my cigars with belly-bands, and then tip the word to him. He smells the cigars and says: "Have you got any more of them?"

"Another good handful," I say, "and my comrade," I point to Kropp, "he has some as well. We might possibly be glad to hand them to you out of the window of the hospital train in the morning."

He understands, of course, smells them once again and says: "Done."

We cannot get a minute's sleep all night. Seven fellows die in our ward. One of them sings hymns in a high cracked tenor before he begins to gurgle. Another has crept out of his bed to the window. He lies in front of it as though he wants to look out for the last time.

188

Our stretchers stand on the platform. We wait for the train. It rains and the station has no roof. Our covers are thin. We have already waited two hours.

The sergeant-major looks after us like a mother. Although I feel pretty bad I do not let our scheme out of my mind. Occasionally I let him see the packet and give him one cigar in advance. In exchange the sergeant-major covers us over with a waterproof sheet.

"Albert, old man, I suddenly bethink myself, our four-poster and the cat – "

"And the club chairs," he adds.

Yes, the club chairs with red plush. In the evening we used to sit in them like lords, and intended later on to let them out by the hour. One cigarette per hour. It might have turned into a regular business, a real good living.

"And our bags of grub, too, Albert."

We grow melancholy. We might have made some use of the things. If only the train left one day later Kat would be sure to find us and bring us the stuff.

What damned hard luck! In our bellies there is gruel, mean hospital stuff, and in our bags roast pork. But we are so weak that we cannot work up any more excitement about it.

The stretchers are sopping wet by the time the train arrives in the morning. The sergeant-major sees to it that we are put in the same car. There is a crowd of Red Cross nurses. Kropp is stowed in below. I am lifted up and put into the bed above him.

"Good God!" I exclaim suddenly.

"What is it?" asks the sister.

I cast a glance at the bed. It is covered with clean snow-white linen, that even has the marks of the iron still on it. And my shirt has gone six weeks without being washed and is terribly muddy.

"Can't you get in by yourself?" asks the sister gently.

"Why yes," I say in a sweat, "but take off the bed-cover first."

"What for?"

I feel like a pig. Must I get in there? – "It will get – " I hesitate.

"A little bit dirty?" she suggests helpfully. "That doesn't matter, we will wash it again afterwards."

"No, no, not that – " I say excitedly. I am not equal to such overwhelming refinement.

"When you have been lying out there in the trenches, surely we can wash a sheet," she goes on.

I look at her, she is young and crisp, spotless and neat, like everything here; a man cannot realize that it isn't for officers only, and feels himself strange and in some way even alarmed.

All the same, the woman is a tormentor, she is going to force me to say it. "It is only – " I try again, surely she must know what I mean.

"What is it then?"

"Because of the lice," I bawl out at last.

She laughs. "Well, they must have a good day for once, too."

Now I don't care any more. I scramble into bed and pull up the covers.

A hand gropes over the bed-cover. The sergeant-major. He goes off with the cigars.

190

An hour later we notice that we are moving.

At night I cannot sleep. Kropp is restless too. The train rides easily over the rails. I cannot realize it all yet; a bed, a train, home. "Albert!" I whisper.

"Yes – "

"Do you know where the latrine is?"

"Over to the right of the door, I think."

"I'm going to have a look." It is dark, I grope for the edge of the bed and cautiously try to slide down. But my foot finds no support, I begin to slip, the plaster leg is no help, and with a crash I lie on the floor.

"Damn!" I say.

"Have you bumped yourself?" asks Kropp.

"You could hear that well enough for yourself," I growl, "my head – "

A door opens in the rear of the car. The sister comes with a light and looks at me.

"He has fallen out of bed – "

She feels my pulse and smooths my forehead. "You haven't any fever, though."

"No," I agree.

"Have you been dreaming then?" she asks.

"Perhaps – " I evade. The interrogation starts again. She looks at me with her clear eyes, and the more wonderful and sweet she is the less am I able to tell her what I want.

I am lifted up into bed again. That will be all right. As soon as she goes I must try to climb down again. If she were an old woman, it might be easier to say what a man wants, but she is so very young, at the most twenty-five, it can't be done, I cannot possibly tell her.

Then Albert comes to my rescue, he is not bashful, it makes no difference to him who is upset. He calls to the sister. She turns round. "Sister, he wants – " but no more does Albert know how to express it

191

modestly and decently. Out there we say it in a single word, but here, to such a lady – All at once he remembers his school days and finishes hastily: "He wants to leave the room, sister."

"Ah!" says the sister, "but he shouldn't climb out of his bed with his plaster bandage. What do you want then?" she says, turning to me.

I am in mortal terror at this new turn, for I haven't any idea what the things are called professionally. She comes to my help.

"Little or big?"

This shocking business! I sweat like a pig and say shyly: "Well, only quite a little one – "

At any rate, it produces the effect.

I get a bottle. After a few hours I am no longer the only one, and by morning we are quite accustomed to it and ask for what we want without any false modesty.

The train travels slowly. Sometimes it halts and the dead are unloaded. It halts often.

Albert is feverish. I feel miserable and have a good deal of pain, but the worst of it is that apparently there are still lice under the plaster bandage. They itch terribly, and I cannot scratch myself.

We sleep through the days. The country glides quietly past the window. The third night we reach Herstal. I hear from the sister that Albert is to be put off at the next station because of his fever. "How far does the train go?" I ask.

"To Cologne."

"Albert," I say, "we stick together; you see."

On the sister's next round I hold my breath and press it up into my head. My face swells and turns red. She stops. "Are you in pain?"

"Yes," I groan, "all of a sudden."

She gives me a thermometer and goes on. I would not have been under Kat's tuition if I did not know what to do now. These army thermometers are not made for old soldiers. All one has to do is to

192

drive the quicksilver up and then it stays there without falling again.

I stick the thermometer under my arm at a slant, and flip it steadily with my forefinger. Then I give it a shake. I send it up to 100.2°. But that is not enough. A match held cautiously near to it brings it up to 101.6°.

As the sister comes back, I blow myself out, breathe in short gasps, goggle at her with vacant eyes, toss about restlessly, and mutter in a whisper: "I can't bear it any longer – "

She notes me down on a slip of paper. I know perfectly well my plaster bandage will not be re-opened if it can be avoided.

Albert and I are put off together.

We are in the same room in a Catholic Hospital. That is a piece of luck, the Catholic infirmaries are noted for their good treatment and good food. The hospital has been filled up from our train, there are a great many bad cases amongst them. We do not get examined to-day because there are too few surgeons. The flat trolleys with the rubber wheels pass continuously along the corridor, and always with someone stretched at full length upon them. A damnable position, stretched out at full length like that; – the only time it is good is when one is asleep.

The night is very disturbed. No one can sleep. Toward morning we doze a little. I wake up just as it grows light. The door stands open and I hear voices from the corridor. The others wake up too. One fellow, who has been there a couple of days already, explains it to us: "Up here in the corridor every morning the sisters say prayers. They call it Morning Devotion. And so that you can get your share, they leave the door open."

No doubt it is well meant, but it gives us aches in our heads and bones.

"Such an absurdity!" I say, "just when a man drops off to sleep."

"All the light cases are up here, that's why they do it here," he replies.

Albert groans. I get furious and call out: "Be quiet out there!"

A minute later a sister appears. In her black and white dress she looks like a beautiful tea-cosy. "Shut the door, will you, sister?" says someone.

"We are saying prayers, that is why the door is open," she responds.

"But we want to go on sleeping—"

"Prayer is better than sleep," she stands there and smiles innocently. "And it is seven o'clock already."

Albert groans again. "Shut the door," I snort.

She is quite disconcerted. Apparently she cannot understand. "But we are saying prayers for you too."

"Shut the door, anyway."

She disappears, leaving the door open. The intoning of the Litany proceeds.

I feel savage, and say: "I'm going to count up to three. If it doesn't stop before then I'll let something fly."

"Me, too," says another.

I count up to five. Then I take hold of a bottle, aim, and heave it through the door into the corridor. It smashes into a thousand pieces. The praying stops. A swarm of sisters appear and reproach us in concert.

"Shut the door!" we yell.

They withdraw. The little one who came first is the last to go. "Heathen," she chirps, but shuts the door all the same. We have won.

194

At noon the hospital inspector arrives and abuses us. He threatens us with clink and all the rest of it. But a hospital inspector is just the same as a commissariat inspector, or anyone else who wears a long dagger and shoulder straps, but is really a clerk, and is never considered even by a recruit as a real officer. So we let him talk. What can they do to us, anyway –

"Who threw the bottle?" he asks.

Before I can think whether I should report myself, someone says: "I did."

A man with a bristling beard sits up. Everyone is excited; why should he report himself?

"You?"

"Yes. I was annoyed because we were waked up unnecessarily and lost my senses so that I did not know what I was doing."

195

He talks like a book.

"What is your name?"

"Reinforcement-Reservist Josef Hamacher."

The inspector departs.

We are all curious. "But why did you say you did it? It wasn't you at all!"

He grins. "That doesn't matter. I have a shooting license."

Then, of course, we all understand. Whoever has a shooting license can do just whatever he pleases.

"Yes," he explains, "I got a crack in the head and they presented me with a certificate to say that I was periodically not responsible for my actions. Ever since then I've had a grand time. No one dares to annoy me. And nobody does anything to me.

"I reported myself because the shot amused me. If they open the door again to-morrow we will pitch another."

We are overjoyed. With Josef Hamacher in our midst we can now risk anything.

Then come the soundless, flat trollies to take us away.

The bandages are stuck fast. We bellow like steers.

There are eight men in our room. Peter, a curly-black-haired fellow, has the worst injury; – a severe lung wound. Franz Wächter, alongside him, has a shot in the arm which didn't look too bad at first. But the third night he calls out to us, telling us to ring, he thinks he has a hæmorrhage.

I ring loudly. The night sister does not come. We have been making rather heavy demands on her during the night, because we have all been freshly bandaged, and so have a good deal of pain. One wants his leg placed so, another so, a third wants water, a fourth wants her to shake up his pillow; – in the end the buxom old body grumbled bad-temperedly and slammed the doors. Now no doubt

196

she thinks it is something of the same sort and so she is not coming.

We wait. Then Franz says: "Ring again."

I do so. Still she does not put in an appearance. In our wing there is only one night sister, perhaps she has something to do in one of the other rooms. "Franz, are you quite sure you are bleeding?" I ask. "Otherwise we shall be getting cursed again."

"The bandage is wet. Can't anybody make a light?"

That cannot be done either. The switch is by the door and none of us can stand up. I hold my thumb against the button of the bell till it becomes numb. Perhaps the sister has fallen asleep. They certainly have a great deal to do and are overworked day after day. And added to that is the everlasting praying.

"Should we smash a bottle?" asks Josef Hamacher of the shooting license.

"She wouldn't hear that any more than the bell."

At last the door opens. The old lady appears, mumbling. When she perceives Franz's trouble she begins to bustle, and says: "Why did not someone say I was wanted?"

"We did ring. And none of us here can walk."

He has been bleeding badly and she binds him up. In the morning we look at his face, it has become sharp and yellow, whereas the evening before he looked almost healthy. Now a sister comes oftener.

Sometimes there are Red Cross voluntary-aid sisters. They are pleasant, but often rather unskilled. They frequently give us pain when re-making our beds, and then are so frightened that they hurt us still more.

The nuns are more reliable. They know how they must take hold of us, but we would be more pleased if they were somewhat more cheerful. A few of them have real spirit, they are superb. There is no one who would not do anything for Sister Libertine, this marvellous sister, who spreads good cheer through the whole wing even when she can only be seen in the distance. And there are others like her. We would go through fire for her. A man cannot really complain, here he is treated by the nuns exactly like a civilian. On the other hand, just to think of a garrison hospital gives a man the creeps.

Franz Wächter does not regain his strength. One day he is taken away and does not come back. Josef Hamacher knows all about it: "We shan't see him again. They have put him in the Dead Room."

"What do you mean, Dead Room?" asks Kropp.

"Well, Dying Room – "

"What is that, then?"

"A little room at the corner of the building. Whoever is about to kick the bucket is put in there. There are two beds in it. It is generally called the Dying Room."

"But what do they do that for?"

"They don't have so much work to do afterwards. It is more convenient, too, because it lies right beside the lift to the mortuary. Perhaps also they do it for the sake of the others, so that no one in the ward dies in sympathy. And they can look after him better, too, if he is by himself."

"But what about him?"

Josef shrugs his shoulders. "Usually he doesn't take much notice any more."

"Does everybody know about it then?"

"Anyone who has been here long enough knows, of course."

In the afternoon Franz Wächter's bed has a fresh occupant. A couple of days later they take the new man away, too. Josef makes a significant gesture. We see many come and go.

Often relatives sit by the beds and weep or talk softly and awkwardly. One old woman will not go away, but she cannot stay there the whole night through. Another morning she comes very early, but not early enough; for as she goes up to the bed, someone else is in it already. She has to go to the mortuary. The apples that she has brought with her she gives to us.

And then little Peter begins to get worse. His temperature chart looks bad, and one day the flat trolley stands beside his bed. "Where to?" he asks.

"To the bandaging ward."

He is lifted out. But the sister makes the mistake of removing his tunic from the hook and putting it on the trolley too, so that she should not have to make two journeys. Peter understands immediately and tries to roll off the trolley. "I'm stopping here!"

They push him back. He cries out feebly with his shattered lung. "I won't go to the Dying Room."

"But we are going to the bandaging ward."

"Then what do you want my tunic for?" He can speak no more. Hoarse, agitated, he whispers: "Stopping here!"

They do not answer but wheel him out. At the door he tries to raise himself up. His black curly head sways, his eyes are full of tears. "I will come back again! I will come back again!" he cries.

The door shuts. We are all excited; but we say nothing. At last Josef says: "Many a man has said that. Once a man is in there, he never comes through."

I am operated on and vomit for two days. My bones will not grow together, so the surgeon's secretary says. Another fellow's have grown crooked; his are broken again. It is disgusting.

Among our new arrivals there are two young soldiers with flat feet. The chief surgeon discovers them on his rounds, and is overjoyed. "We'll soon put that right," he tells them, "we will just do a small operation, and then you will have perfectly sound feet. Enter them down, sister."

As soon as he is gone, Josef, who knows everything, warns them: "Don't you let him operate on you! That is a special scientific stunt of the old boy's. He goes absolutely crazy whenever he can get hold of anyone to do it on. He operates on you for flat feet, and there's no mistake, you don't have them any more; you have club feet instead, and have to walk all the rest of your life on sticks."

"What should a man do, then?" asks one of them.

"Say No. You are here to be cured of your wound, not your flat feet. Did you have any trouble with them in the field? No, well, there you are! At present you can still walk, but if once the old boy gets you under the knife you'll be cripples. What he wants is little dogs to experiment with, so the war is a glorious time for him, as it is for all the surgeons. You take a look down below at the staff; there are a dozen fellows hobbling around that he has operated on. A lot of them have been here all the time since 'fourteen and 'fifteen. Not a single one of them can walk better than he could before, almost all of them worse, and most only with plaster legs. Every six months he catches them again and breaks their bones afresh, and every time is going to be the successful one. You take my word, he won't dare to do it if you say No."

200

"Ach, man," says one of the two unfortunates, "better your feet than your brain-box. There's no telling what you'll get if you go back out there again. They can do with me just as they please, so long as I get back home. Better to have a club foot than be dead."

The other, a young fellow like ourselves, won't have it done. One morning the old man has the two hauled up and lectures and jaws at them so long, that in the end they consent. What else could they do? – They are mere privates, and he is a big bug. They are brought back chloroformed and plastered.

It is going badly with Albert. They have taken him and amputated his leg. The whole leg has been taken off from the thigh. Now he hardly speaks any more. Once he says he will shoot himself the first time he can get hold of his revolver again.

A new convoy arrives. Our room gets two blind men. One of them is a very youthful musician. The sisters never have a knife with them when they feed him; he has already snatched one from a sister. But in spite of this caution there is an incident. In the evening, while he is being fed, the sister is called away, and leaves the plate with the fork on his table. He gropes for the fork, seizes it and drives it with all his force against his heart, then he snatches up a shoe and strikes with it against the handle as hard as he can. We call for help and three men are necessary to take the fork away from him. The blunt prongs had already penetrated deep. He abuses us all night so that no one can go to sleep. In the morning he has lock-jaw.

Again beds become empty. Day after day goes by with pain and fear, groans and death-gurgles. Even the Death Room is no use any more, it is too small; fellows die during the night in our room. They go even faster than the sisters can cope with them.

But one day the door flies open, the flat trolley rolls in, and there on the stretcher, pale, thin, upright and triumphant, with his shaggy

201

head of curls sits Peter. Sister Libertine with beaming looks pushes him over to his former bed. He is back from the Dying Room. We have long supposed him dead.

He looks round: "What do you say now?"

And even Josef has to admit that it is the first time he has ever known of such a thing.

Gradually a few of us venture to stand up. And I am given crutches to hobble around on. But I do not make much use of them; I cannot bear Albert's gaze as I move about the room. His eyes always follow me with such a strange look. So I sometimes escape to the corridor; – there I can move about more freely.

On the next floor below are the abdominal and spine cases, head wounds and double amputations. On the right side of the wing are the jaw wounds, gas cases, nose, ear, and neck wounds. On the left the blind and the lung wounds, pelvis wounds, wounds in the joints, wounds in the testicles, wounds in the intestines. Here a man realizes for the first time in how many places a man can get hit.

Two fellows die of tetanus. Their skin turns pale, their limbs stiffen, at last only their eyes live – stubbornly. Many of the wounded have their shattered limbs hanging free in the air from a gallows; underneath the wound a basin is placed into which the pus drips. Every two or three hours the vessel is emptied. Other men lie in stretching bandages with heavy weights hanging from the end of the bed. I see intestine wounds that are constantly full of excreta. The surgeon's clerk shows me X-ray photographs of completely smashed hip-bones, knees, and shoulders.

A man cannot realize that above such shattered bodies there are still human faces in which life goes its daily round. And this is only one hospital, one single station; there are hundreds of thousands in Germany, hundreds of thousands in France, hundreds of thousands in Russia. How senseless is everything that can ever be written, done, or thought, when such things are possible. It must all be lies and of no account when the culture of a thousand years could not prevent this stream of blood being poured out, these torture-chambers in their hundreds of thousands. A hospital alone shows what war is.

I am young, I am twenty years old; yet I know nothing of life but despair, death, fear, and fatuous superficiality cast over an abyss of sorrow. I see how peoples are set against one another, and in silence, unknowingly, foolishly, obediently, innocently slay one another. I see that the keenest brains of the world invent weapons and words to make it yet more refined and enduring. And all men of my age, here and over there, throughout the whole world, see these things; all my generation is experiencing these things with me. What would our fathers do if we suddenly stood up and came before them and proffered our account? What do they expect of us if a time ever comes when the war is over? Through the years our business has been killing;—it was our first calling in life. Our knowledge of life is limited to death. What will happen afterwards? And what shall come out of us?

After a few weeks I have to go each morning to the massage department. There my leg is harnessed up and made to move. The arm has healed long since.

New convoys arrive from the line. The bandages are no longer made of cloth, but of white crêpe paper. Rag bandages have become scarce at the front.

Albert's stump heals well. The wound is almost closed. In a few weeks he should go off to an institute for artificial limbs. He continues not to talk much, and is much more solemn than formerly. He often breaks off in his speech and stares in front of him. If he were not here with us he would have shot himself long ago. But now he is over the worst of it, and he often looks on while we play skat.

I get convalescent leave.

My mother does not want to let me go away. She is so feeble. It is all much worse than it was last time.

Then I am sent on from the base and return once more to the line.

Parting from my friend Albert Kropp was very hard. But a man gets used to that sort of thing in the army.

Chapter Eleven

WE COUNT THE WEEKS no more. It was winter when I came up, and when the shells exploded the frozen clods of earth were just as dangerous as the fragments. Now the trees are green again. Our life alternates between billets and the front. We have almost grown accustomed to it; war is a cause of death like cancer and tuberculosis, like influenza and dysentery. The deaths are merely more frequent, more varied and terrible.

Our thoughts are clay, they are moulded with the changes of the days; – when we are resting they are good; under fire, they are dead. Fields of craters within and without.

Everyone is so, not only ourselves here – the things that existed before are no longer valid, and one practically knows them no more. Distinctions, breeding, education are changed, are almost blotted out and hardly recognizable any longer. Sometimes they give an advantage for profiting by a situation; – but they also bring consequences along with them, in that they arouse prejudices which have to be overcome. It is as though formerly we were coins of different provinces; and now we are melted down, and all bear the same stamp. To re-discover the old distinctions, the metal itself must be tested. First we are soldiers and afterwards, in a strange and shamefaced fashion, individual men as well.

It is a great brotherhood, which to a condition of life arising out of the midst of danger, out of the tension and forlornness of death, adds something of the good-fellowship of the folk-song, of the feeling of solidarity of convicts, and of the desperate loyalty to one another of men condemned to death – seeking in a wholly unpathetic way a fleeting enjoyment of the hours as they come. If one wants to appraise it, it is at once heroic and banal – but who wants to do that?

It is this, for example, that makes Tjaden spoon down his ham-and-pea soup in such tearing haste when an enemy attack is reported, simply because he cannot be sure that in an hour's time he will still be alive. We have discussed at length, whether it is right or not to do so. Kat condemns it, because, he says, a man has to reckon with the possibility of an abdominal wound, and that is more dangerous on a full stomach than on an empty one.

Such things are real problems, they are serious matters to us, they cannot be otherwise. Here, on the borders of death, life follows an amazingly simple course, it is limited to what is most necessary, all else lies buried in gloomy sleep; – in that lies our primitiveness and our survival. Were we more subtly differentiated we must long since have gone mad, have deserted, or have fallen. As in a polar expedition, every expression of life must serve only the preservation of existence, and is absolutely focussed on that. All else is banished because it would consume energies unnecessarily. That is the only way to save ourselves. In the quiet hours when the puzzling reflection of former days, like a blurred mirror, projects beyond me the figure of my present existence, I often sit over against myself, as before a stranger, and wonder how the unnamable active principle that calls itself Life has adapted itself even to this form. All other expressions lie in a winter sleep, life is simply one continual watch against the menace of death; – it has transformed us into unthinking animals in order to give us the weapon of instinct – it has reinforced us with dullness, so that we do not go to pieces before the horror, which would overwhelm us if we had clear, conscious thought – it has awakened in us the sense of comradeship, so that we escape the abyss of solitude – it has lent us the indifference of wild creatures, so that in spite of all we perceive the positive in every moment, and store it up as a reserve against the onslaught of nothingness. Thus we live a closed, hard existence of the utmost superficiality, and rarely does an incident strike out a spark. But then unexpectedly a flame of grievous and terrible yearning flares up.

Those are the dangerous moments. They show us that the adjustment is only artificial, that it is not simple rest, but sharpest struggle for rest. In the outward form of our life we are hardly distinguishable from Bushmen; but whereas the latter can be so always, because they are so truly, and at best may develop further by exertion of their spiritual forces, with us it is the reverse; – our inner forces are not exerted toward regeneration, but toward degeneration. The Bushmen are primitive and naturally so, but we are primitive in an artificial sense, and by virtue of the utmost effort.

206

And at night, waking out of a dream, overwhelmed and bewitched by the crowding faces, a man perceives with alarm how slight is the support, how thin the boundary that divides him from the darkness. We are little flames poorly sheltered by frail walls against the storm of dissolution and madness, in which we flicker and sometimes almost go out. Then the muffled roar of the battle becomes a ring that encircles us, we creep in upon ourselves, and with big eyes stare into the night. Our only comfort is the steady breathing of our comrades asleep, and thus we wait for the morning.

Every day and every hour, every shell and every death cuts into this thin support, and the years waste it rapidly. I see how it is already gradually breaking down around me.

There is the mad story of Detering.

He was one of those who kept himself to himself. His misfortune was that he saw a cherry tree in a garden. We were just coming back from the front-line, and at a turning of the road near our new billets, marvellous in the morning twilight, stood this cherry tree before us. It had no leaves, but was one white mass of blossom.

In the evening Detering was not to be seen. Then at last he came back and had a couple of branches of cherry blossom in his hand. We made fun of him, and asked whether he was going to a wedding. He made no answer, but laid them on his bed. During the night I heard him making a noise, he seemed to be packing. I sensed something amiss and went over to him. He made out it was nothing, and I said to him: "Don't do anything silly, Detering."

"Ach, why – it's merely that I can't sleep – "

"What did you pick the cherry branches for?"

"I might have been going to get some more cherry branches," he replied, evasively – and after a while: "I have a big orchard with cherry trees at home. When they are in blossom, from the hay loft they look like one single sheet, so white. It is just the time."

"Perhaps you will get leave soon. You may even be sent back as a farmer."

He nodded, but he was far away. When these peasants are excited they have a curious expression, a mixture of cow and yearning god, half stupid and half rapt. In order to turn him away from his thoughts I asked him for a piece of bread. He gave it to me without a murmur. That was suspicious, for he is usually tight-fisted. So I stayed awake. Nothing happened; in the morning he was as usual.

Apparently he had noticed that I had been watching him; – but the second morning after he was gone. I noticed it but said nothing, in order to give him time; he might perhaps get through. Various fellows have already got into Holland.

But at roll call he was missed. A week after we heard that he had been caught by the field gendarmes, those despicable military police. He had headed toward Germany, that was hopeless, of course – and, of course, he did everything else just as idiotically. Anyone might have known that his flight was only home-sickness and a momentary aberration. But what does a court-martial hundreds of miles behind the front-line know about it? We have heard nothing more of Detering.

But sometimes it broke out in other ways, this danger, these pent-up

208

things, as from an overheated boiler. It will be enough to tell how Berger met his end.

Our trenches have now for some time been shot to pieces, and we have an elastic line, so that there is practically no longer any proper trench warfare. When attack and counter-attack have waged backwards and forwards there remains a broken line and a bitter struggle from crater to crater. The front-line has been penetrated, and everywhere small groups have established themselves, the fight is carried on from clusters of shell-holes.

We are in a crater, the English are coming down obliquely, they are turning our flank and working in behind us. We are surrounded. It is not easy to surrender, fog and smoke hang over us, no one would recognize that we wanted to give ourselves up, and perhaps we don't want to, a man doesn't even know himself at such moments. We hear the explosions of the hand-grenades coming toward us. Our machine-gun sweeps over the semicircle in front of us. The cooling-water evaporates, we hastily pass round the case, every man urinates in it, and thus we again have water, and are able to continue firing. But behind us the attack crashes ever nearer.

A few minutes and we are lost.

Then, at closest range, a second machine-gun bursts out. It is set up in a crater alongside us; Berger has fetched it, and now the counter-attack comes over from behind; we are set free and make contact with the rear.

Afterwards, as we lie in comparatively good cover, one of the food-carriers reports that a couple of hundred yards distant there lies a wounded messenger-dog.

"Where?" asks Berger.

The other describes the place to him. Berger goes off either to fetch the beast in or to shoot it. Six months ago he would not have cared, he would have been reasonable. We try to prevent him. Then, as he goes off grimly, all we can say is: "You're mad," and let him go. For these cases of front-line madness become dangerous if one is not able to fling the man to the ground and hold him fast. And Berger is six feet and the most powerful man in the company.

He is absolutely mad for he has to pass through the barrage; but this lightning that lowers somewhere above us all has struck him and made him demented. It affects others so that they begin to rave, to run away – there was one man who even tried to dig himself into the ground with hands, feet, and teeth.

It is true, such things are often simulated, but the pretence itself is a symptom. Berger, who means to finish off the dog, is carried off with a wound in the pelvis, and one of the fellows who carry him gets a bullet in the cheek while doing it.

Müller is dead. Someone shot him point blank in the stomach with a Very light. He lived for half an hour, quite conscious, and in terrible pain.

Before he died he handed over his pocketbook to me, and bequeathed me his boots – the same that he once inherited from Kemmerich. I wear them, for they fit me quite well. After me Tjaden will get them, I have promised them to him.

We have been able to bury Müller, but he is not likely to remain long undisturbed. Our lines are falling back. There are too many fresh English and American regiments over there. There's too much corned beef and white wheaten bread. Too many new guns. Too many aeroplanes.

But we are emaciated and starved. Our food is so bad and mixed up with so much substitute stuff that it makes us ill. The factory owners in Germany have grown wealthy; – dysentery dissolves our bowels. The latrine perches are always densely crowded; the people at home ought to be shown these grey, yellow, miserable, wasted faces here, these bent figures from whose bodies the colic wrings out the blood, and who with lips trembling and distorted with pain, grin at one another and say: "It is not much sense pulling up one's trousers again – "

Our artillery is fired out, it has too few shells and the barrels are so worn that they shoot uncertainly, and scatter so widely as even to fall on ourselves. We have too few horses. Our fresh troops are anæmic boys in need of rest, who cannot carry a pack, but merely know how to die. By thousands. They understand nothing about warfare, they simply go on and let themselves be shot down. A single flyer routed two companies of them for a joke, just as they came fresh from the train – before they had ever heard of such a thing as cover.

"Germany ought to be empty soon," says Kat.

We have given up hope that some day an end may come. We never think so far. A man can stop a bullet and be killed; he can get wounded, and then the hospital is his next stop. There, if they do not amputate him, he sooner or later falls into the hands of one of those staff surgeons who, with the War Service Cross in his buttonhole, says to him: "What, one leg a bit short? If you have any pluck you don't need to run at the front. The man is A1. Dismiss!"

Kat tells a story that has travelled the whole length of the front from the Vosges to Flanders; – of the staff surgeon who reads the names on the list, and when a man comes before him, without looking up says: "A1. We need soldiers up there." A fellow with a wooden leg comes up before him, the staff surgeon again says A1 – "And then," Kat raises his voice, "the fellow says to him: 'I already have a wooden leg, but when I go back again and they shoot off my head, then I will get a wooden head made and become a staff surgeon.' " This answer tickles us all immensely.

There may be good doctors, and there are, lots of them; all the same, every soldier some time during his hundreds of inspections falls

211

into the clutches of one of these countless hero-grabbers who pride themselves on changing as many C3's and B3's as possible into A1's.

There are many such stories, they are mostly far more bitter. All the same, they have nothing to do with mutiny or lead-swinging. They are merely honest and call a thing by its name; for there is a very great deal of fraud, injustice, and baseness in the army. — Is it nothing that regiment after regiment returns again and again to the ever more hopeless struggle, that attack follows attack along the weakening, retreating, crumbling line?

From a mockery the tanks have become a terrible weapon. Armoured they come rolling on in long lines, and more than anything else embody for us the horror of war.

We do not see the guns that bombard us; the attacking lines of the enemy infantry are men like ourselves; but these tanks are machines, their caterpillars run on as endless as the war, they are annihilation, they roll without feeling into the craters, and climb up again without stopping, a fleet of roaring, smoke-belching armour-clads, invulnerable steel beasts squashing the dead and the wounded — we shrivel up in our thin skin before them, against their colossal weight our arms are sticks of straw, and our hand-grenades matches.

Shells, gas clouds, and flotillas of tanks — shattering, starvation, death.

Dysentery, influenza, typhus — murder, burning, death.

Trenches, hospitals, the common grave — there are no other possibilities.

In one attack our company commander, Bertinck, falls. He was one of those superb front-line officers who are foremost in every hot place. He was with us for two years without being wounded, so that something had to happen in the end.

We occupy a crater and get surrounded. The stink of petroleum or oil blows across with the fumes of powder. Two fellows with a flame-thrower are seen, one carries the tin on his back, the other has the hose in his hands from which the fire spouts. If they get so near that they can reach us we are done for, we cannot retreat yet.

We open fire on them. But they work nearer and things begin to look bad. Bertinck is lying in the hole with us. When he sees that we cannot escape because under the sharp fire we must make the most of this cover, he takes a rifle, crawls out of the hole, and lying down propped on his elbows, he takes aim. He fires – the same moment a bullet smacks into him, they have got him. Still he lies and aims again;

213

– once he shifts and again takes his aim; at last the rifle cracks. Bertinck lets the gun drop and says: "Good," and slips back into the hole. The hindermost of the two flame-throwers is hit, he falls, the hose slips away from the other fellow, the fire squirts about on all sides and the man burns.

Bertinck has a chest wound. After a while a fragment smashes away his chin, and the same fragment has sufficient force to tear open Leer's hip. Leer groans as he supports himself on his arm, he bleeds quickly, no one can help him. Like an emptying tube, after a couple of minutes he collapses.

What use is it to him now that he was such a good mathematician at school?

The months pass by. The summer of 1918 is the most bloody and the most terrible. The days stand like angels in gold and blue, incomprehensible, above the ring of annihilation. Every man here knows that we are losing the war. Not much is said about it, we are falling back, we will not be able to attack again after this big offensive, we have no more men and no more ammunition.

Still the campaign goes on – the dying goes on –

Summer of 1918 – Never has life in its niggardliness seemed to us so desirable as now; – the red poppies in the meadows round our billets, the smooth beetles on the blades of grass, the warm evenings in the cool, dim rooms, the black, mysterious trees of the twilight, the stars and the flowing waters, dreams and long sleep –. O Life, life, life!

Summer of 1918 – Never was so much silently suffered as in the moment when we depart once again for the front-line. Wild, tormenting rumours of an armistice and peace are in the air, they lay hold on our hearts and make the return to the front harder than ever.

Summer of 1918 – Never was life in the line more bitter and more full of horror than in the hours of the bombardment, when the blanched faces lie in the dirt, and the hands clutch at the one thought: No! No! Not now! Not now at the last moment!

Summer of 1918 – Breath of hope that sweeps over the scorched fields, raging fever of impatience, of disappointment, of the most agonizing terror of death, insensate question: Why? Why do they not make an end? And why do these rumours of an end fly about?

There are so many airmen here, and they are so sure of themselves that they give chase to single individuals, just as though they were hares. For every one German plane there come at least five English and American. For one hungry, wretched German soldier come five of the enemy, fresh and fit. For one German army loaf there are fifty tins of canned beef over there. We are not beaten, for as soldiers we are better and more experienced; we are simply crushed and driven back by overwhelmingly superior forces.

Behind us lie rainy weeks – grey sky, grey fluid earth, grey dying. If we go out, the rain at once soaks through overcoats and clothing; – and we remain wet all the time we are in the line. We never get dry. Those who still wear high boots tie sand bags round the top so that the mud does not pour in so fast. The rifles are caked, the uniforms caked, everything is fluid and dissolved, the earth one dripping, soaked, oily mass in which lie the yellow pools with red spiral streams

215

of blood and into which the dead, wounded, and survivors slowly sink down.

The storm lashes us, out of the confusion of grey and yellow the hail of splinters whips forth the childlike cries of the wounded, and in the night shattered life groans wearily to the silence.

Our hands are earth, our bodies clay and our eyes pools of rain. We do not know whether we still live.

Then the heat sinks heavily into our shell-holes like a jelly-fish, moist and oppressive, and on one of these late summer days, while bringing food, Kat falls. We two are alone. I bind up his wound; his shin seems to be smashed. It has got the bone, and Kat groans desperately: "At last – just at the last – "

I comfort him. "Who knows how long the mess will go on yet! Now you are saved – "

The wound begins to bleed fast. Kat cannot be left by himself while

216

I try to find a stretcher. Anyway, I don't know of a stretcher-bearer's post in the neighbourhood.

Kat is not very heavy; so I take him up on my back and start off to the dressing-station with him.

Twice we rest. He suffers acutely on the way. We do not speak much. I have opened the collar of my tunic and breathe heavily, I sweat and my face is swollen with the strain of carrying. All the same I urge him to let us go on, for the place is dangerous.

"Shall we go on again, Kat?"

"Must, Paul."

"Then come."

I raise him up, he stands on the uninjured leg and supports himself against a tree. I take up the wounded leg carefully, then he gives a jump and I take the knee of the sound leg also under my arm.

The going is more difficult. Often a shell whistles across. I go as quickly as I can, for the blood from Kat's wound drips to the ground. We cannot shelter ourselves properly from the explosions; before we can take cover the danger is all over.

We lie down in a small shell-hole to rest. I give Kat some tea from my water bottle. We smoke a cigarette. "Well, Kat," I say gloomily, "we are going to be separated at last."

He is silent and looks at me.

"Do you remember, Kat, how we commandeered the goose? And how you brought me out of the barrage when I was still a young recruit and was wounded for the first time? I cried then. Kat, that is almost three years ago."

He nods.

The anguish of solitude rises up in me. When Kat is taken away I will not have one friend left.

"Kat, in any case we must see one another again, if it is peace time before you come back."

"Do you think that I will be marked A1 again with this leg?" he asks bitterly.

"With rest it will get better. The joint is all right. It may limp a bit."

"Give me another cigarette," he says.

"Perhaps we could do something together later on, Kat." I am very miserable, it is impossible that Kat — Kat my friend, Kat with the drooping shoulders and the poor, thin moustache, Kat, whom I know as I know no other man, Kat with whom I have shared these years — it is impossible that perhaps I shall not see Kat again.

"In any case give me your address at home, Kat. And here is mine, I will write it down for you."

I write his address in my pocketbook. How forlorn I am already, though he still sits here beside me. Couldn't I shoot myself quickly in the foot so as to be able to go with him?

Suddenly Kat gurgles and turns green and yellow. "Let us go on," he stammers.

I jump up, eager to help him, I take him up and start off at a run, a slow steady pace, so as not to jolt his leg too much.

My throat is parched; everything dances red and black before my eyes, I stagger on doggedly and pitilessly and at last reach the dressing-station.

There I drop down on my knees, but have still enough strength to fall on to the side where Kat's sound leg is. After a few minutes I straighten myself up again. My legs and my hands tremble. I have trouble in finding my water bottle, to take a pull. My lips tremble as I try to drink. But I smile — Kat is saved.

After a while I begin to sort out the confusion of voices that falls on my ears.

"You might have spared yourself that," says an orderly.

I look at him without comprehending.

He points to Kat. "He is stone dead."

218

I do not understand him. "He has been hit in the shin," I say.

The orderly stands still. "That as well."

I turn round. My eyes are still dulled, the sweat breaks out on me again, it runs over my eyelids. I wipe it away and peer at Kat. He lies still. "Fainted," I say quickly.

The orderly whistles softly. "I know better than that. He is dead. I'll lay any money on that."

I shake my head: "Not possible. Only ten minutes ago I was talking to him. He has fainted."

Kat's hands are warm, I pass my arm under his shoulders in order to rub his temples with some tea. I feel my fingers become moist. As I draw them away from behind his head, they are bloody. "You see – " The orderly whistles once more through his teeth.

On the way without my having noticed it, Kat has caught a splinter in the head. There is just one little hole, it must have been a very tiny, stray splinter. But it has sufficed. Kat is dead.

Slowly I get up.

"Would you like to take his pay-book and his things?" the lance-corporal asks me.

I nod, and he gives them to me.

The orderly is mystified. "You are not related, are you?"

No, we are not related. No, we are not related.

Do I walk? Have I feet still? I raise my eyes, I let them move round, and turn myself with them, one circle, one circle, and I stand in the midst. All is as usual. Only the Militiaman Stanislaus Katczinsky has died.

Then I know nothing more.

219

Chapter Twelve

IT IS AUTUMN. There are not many of the old hands left. I am the last of the seven fellows from our class.

Everyone talks of peace and armistice. All wait. If it again proves an illusion, then they will break up; hope is high, it cannot be taken away again without an upheaval. If there is not peace, then there will be revolution.

I have fourteen days' rest, because I have swallowed a bit of gas; in a little garden I sit the whole day long in the sun. The armistice is coming soon, I believe it now too. Then we will go home.

Here my thoughts stop and will not go any farther. All that meets me, all that floods over me are but feelings – greed of life, love of home, yearning of the blood, intoxication of deliverance. But no aims.

Had we returned home in 1916, out of the suffering and the strength of our experiences we might have unleashed a storm. Now if we go back we will be weary, broken, burnt out, rootless, and without hope. We will not be able to find our way any more.

And men will not understand us – for the generation that grew up before us, though it has passed these years with us here, already had a home and a calling; now it will return to its old occupations, and the war will be forgotten – and the generation that has grown up after us will be strange to us and push us aside. We will be superfluous even to ourselves, we will grow older, a few will adapt themselves, some others will merely submit, and most will be bewildered; – the years will pass by and in the end we shall fall into ruin.

But perhaps all this that I think is mere melancholy and dismay, which will fly away as the dust, when I stand once again beneath the poplars and listen to the rustling of their leaves. It cannot be that it has gone, the yearning that made our blood unquiet, the unknown,

220

the perplexing, the oncoming things, the thousand faces of the future, the melodies from dreams and from books, the whispers and divinations of women, it cannot be that this has vanished in bombardment, in despair, in brothels.

Here the trees show gay and golden, the berries of the rowan stand red among the leaves, country roads run white out to the sky-line, and the canteens hum like beehives with rumours of peace.

I stand up.

I am very quiet. Let the months and years come, they bring me nothing more, they can bring me nothing more. I am so alone, and so without hope that I can confront them without fear. The life that has borne me through these years is still in my hands and my eyes. Whether I have subdued it, I know not. But so long as it is there it will seek its own way out, heedless of the will that is within me.

He fell in October, 1918, on a day that was so quiet and still on the whole front, that the army report confined itself to the single sentence: All quiet on the Western Front.

He had fallen forward and lay on the earth as though sleeping. Turning him over one saw that he could not have suffered long; his face had an expression of calm, as though almost glad the end had come.